PUFFIN

The Ma... ...rs

When M... ...g Valley J... ...et for the Jugn... ...ppeal is £100 short, Handles & Spouts Incorporated, or Hands for short, step in.

They decide to organize a jumble sale to raise the final £100. But their publicity is ruined by the wealthy Mrs Hopp-Daniels, with her prize-winning rabbit, Empress Cleopatra. However, due to an oversight, she leaves the strange-looking magician, Mr Amazing, unexpectedly at their disposal. Can he really do anything for them, or is he just making empty promises?

This is the sixth enthralling story about Handles & Spouts and the adventures of its members at Jug Valley Juniors.

Anne Digby was born in Kingston upon Thames, Surrey, but has lived in the West Country for many years. As well as the *Jug Valley* books, she is the author of the popular *Trebizon* and *Me, Jill Robinson* stories.

Alan Davidson's books include the *Annabel* stories and *The Bewitching of Alison Allbright*.

The Magic Man at Jug Valley Juniors

Anne Digby
Story devised with **Alan Davidson**

Illustrated by
Piers Sanford

PUFFIN BOOKS

PUFFIN BOOKS

Published by the Penguin Group
Penguin Books Ltd, 27 Wrights Lane, London W8 5TZ, England
Penguin Books USA Inc., 375 Hudson Street, New York, New York 10014, USA
Penguin Books Australia Ltd, Ringwood, Victoria, Australia
Penguin Books Canada Ltd, 10 Alcorn Avenue, Toronto, Ontario, Canada M4V 3B2
Penguin Books (NZ) Ltd, 182–190 Wairau Road, Auckland 10, New Zealand

Penguin Books Ltd, Registered Offices: Harmondsworth, Middlesex, England

Published in Puffin Books 1993
10 9 8 7 6 5 4 3 2 1

Text copyright © Anne Digby, 1993
Illustrations copyright © Piers Sanford, 1993
All rights reserved

The moral right of the author has been asserted

Typeset by DatIX International Limited, Bungay, Suffolk
Filmset in Monophoto Baskerville
Printed in England by Clays Ltd, St Ives plc

Contents

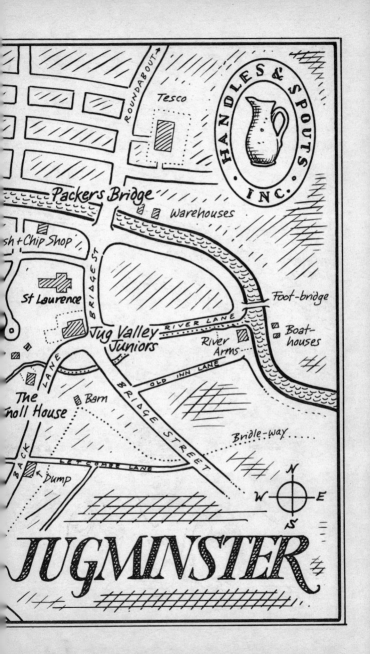

This book is for Maggie

chapter 1

Disaster

*T*he picture of the rabbit on the front page came as a tremendous blow to Handles & Spouts. The other four members of the Jumble Sale committee were equally horror-struck. As for Mr Gage, 6A's class teacher, he felt badly let down. When he saw that front-page story about the rabbit, he wondered if he'd ever again be able to trust his friend, the editor of the *Jugminster Advertiser*.

It was a Friday afternoon. The nine members of Class 6A's fund-raising committee were staying on late with their teacher, to get the school hall ready for their Grand Jumble Sale. This was to take place on the Saturday.

As well as plenty of interesting jumble to sort out, there was to be a home-made sweets stall, a guess-how-many-Smarties-in-the-jar competition and a raffle for some chocolates, donated by Barley's. The committee had worked very hard.

The five friends in the Handles & Spouts Club, Hands for short, were busy setting up the second-hand bookstall, when Gagey walked over and asked for a volunteer.

'*Advertiser* should be up now,' he said, looking at his watch. 'Who'd like to run down to their office?'

'I would, sir!' exclaimed Mini Minter. She ran off, her blonde fringe bobbing. 'Can't wait to get a look at it!'

Tim, Amy, Ben or Ludo would have gone just as fast. The *Jugminster Advertiser*, the town's popular free newspaper, really *mattered*. It arrived at the offices in Bridge Street on Friday afternoons and by nightfall was distributed to every house in the town and read from cover to cover. If you wanted publicity in Jugminster then you had to be in the *Advertiser*, and this week they were going to be the front-page story. Mini vanished through the doors like a bullet from a shotgun. The other four got back to sorting out, on the long trestle-table, all the old books and magazines and comics they'd been given.

The twins, Tim and Amy Dalladay, enjoyed themselves. They spent the next ten minutes putting paperback and hardback books into separate piles. Ben Brown put some comics into their right sequence to make a complete set. Ludo Johnson read out some funny bits from Asterix, followed by a Knock-Knock joke book.

The best thing about it was looking round the hall, watching the other stalls take shape and knowing that the whole thing had been Hands' idea in the first place. Mr Morton, the headmaster, had found himself in a hole – and they were going to get him out of it!

Then suddenly, behind her, Amy heard a little cry. Mini had returned. She was holding two copies of this week's *Advertiser*, hot off the press. She was puffing and panting to get her breath back, her shoulders heaving.

'Mini's got the paper!' exclaimed Kate Roberts eagerly.

'Let's go and have a look at it!' said Emily Brownjohn.

Mr Gage and Marcus King, trying to get a table up for the bric-à-brac stall, let it drop again.

Everybody, in fact, stopped what they
were doing and converged on Mini. But
Amy had taken one look at her best friend's
expression and realized that something was
wrong.

'What's the matter, Min?' she asked
anxiously.

Mini was holding out the papers. She
seemed to be gulping and trying to find her
voice.

'What's *wrong*?' asked Tim impatiently.

'Everything!' moaned Mini. 'We're not
in it. They haven't used the picture of the

14

lifeboat or anything. They haven't printed our story. They haven't even put our advert in!'

'But it was all going on the front page!' exclaimed Mr Gage in great alarm. He took one of the newspapers from Mini, while Tim snatched the other one. 'Surely the picture of the lifeboat's on the front page?'

'There's just a rabbit, sir. A massive great picture of a rabbit. I thought I must be dreaming, sir!'

'A *rabbit*?' said Mr Gage in complete astonishment.

He unrolled his copy of the paper and stared at the picture, while the others all crowded round Tim's copy and stared too. They looked at it and it looked at them. It was a rabbit all right. Its name, apparently, was Empress Cleopatra.

'This is a disaster,' said Class 6A's teacher.

Leaving the nine members of his class to read the other copy of the *Advertiser*, he strode off up the hall with his own.

'Where are you going, sir?' ventured Dom Joshi.

Mr Gage looked back at them, over his shoulder. He seemed to be grinding his

15

teeth with anger.

'To phone the editor, of course!' he rasped.

chapter 2

Ludo's Lateral Thinking

*I*t was exactly a fortnight since Tim had called an emergency club-meeting. Amy and Mini had insisted. The five friends met in the old caravan at the bottom of the Dalladays' orchard, as usual. Once seated round the table in their secret HQ, they pinned on their little jug badges.

'It's about what Mort said in assembly this morning,' Tim announced.

'What, the extra soccer practices?' asked Ben in surprise.

'No, about the Jugmouth Lifeboat Appeal. You know, about there being only sixteen days left. Spouts think we ought to do something. Urgent!'

'What else *can* we do?' inquired Ludo. 'The school's been doing things for months.

I don't know about your parents, but mine say they've given enough.'

'Spouts have had an idea,' Tim explained.

Jug Valley County Junior School had adopted the Lifeboat Appeal as its charity way back in the spring. Mr Morton, the headmaster, had pledged £1000 towards the new lifeboat, on behalf of the school. The lifeboatmen were really counting on it because the cost of building their boat had gone up – the shortfall was exactly £1000.

At first, everyone at Jug Valley Juniors had been really fired up about it. School parties had been shown round the Lifeboat Station, on the quay at Jugmouth. Tim had asked the lifeboatmen questions and looked at the big old boat and all the gear. It was awesome. The men, he discovered, were all volunteers. When the distress signal howled and their telephones rang, they dropped whatever they were doing, day or night, to report for duty – and could be out on a storm-tossed sea in no time. The distress signal, these days, was an ear-piercing siren.

'In the old days, they fired that big cannon on the beach there,' Tim told Ben excitedly.

'I know,' replied Ben. 'Dad says you could hear it go off, even in Jugminster.'

'Like the First World War, then,' said Ludo, who was a great reader. 'The battlefields were in France but the people who lived on the Sussex Downs could hear the cannon-fire sometimes, right across the English Channel.'

It was the old, sepia-tinted photographs that had moved Amy and Mini, of weather-beaten men in sou'westers, lined up in front of a long-ago lifeboat. The Roll of Honour, with the names of crew members lost at sea, in gilt lettering, stirred them deeply. They shouldn't have to put up with a grotty lifeboat. Not when they needed a new one!

But now, after many months, fund-raising had ground to a halt. Parents and friends had been very generous. Class 6B's sponsored swim had raised a lot and some of the younger classes had put on their own events, too. But it was hopeless going back to the same people again and again for the Lifeboat Appeal – not with Oxfam and Poppy Day and all the other things that went on in the town.

'Sadly, it seems we shall *not* reach our target of £1000 for the Jugmouth Lifeboat

Appeal,' the headmaster had told them in assembly. He looked really upset about it. 'You've all made a great effort but we seem to be stuck at just under £900. The Appeal, of course, closes at the end of the month and our cheque must be in by then. If any class has one last bright idea, please speak to your teachers about it. But another £100 is, I fear, beyond us. I know you've all done your best.'

Mr Morton seemed to be bowing to the inevitable. He was bitterly disappointed that the school was unable to honour its pledge of £1000.

But to Amy and Mini it was unthinkable. They discussed it together. The last £100 *must* be raised. Surely it *could* be, especially in view of Mr Gage's special connections, about which by chance they'd just found out.

'It'd have to be a pretty good idea,' Ben was saying, as they sat round the table at HQ. He looked as doubtful as Ludo. 'I don't see how we could raise £100 in sixteen days, all on our own.'

'Not all on our own!' said Mini impatiently. 'Class 6A, we mean. With Mr Gage helping. And not getting money off parents and friends and stuff – but thinking up something the whole town could come to.'

'You see, guess what they've found out,' Tim explained. 'Gagey knows the editor of the *Jugminster Advertiser*. They play snooker together!'

'Ah!' Ludo looked interested. 'That sounds promising. You mean we persuade him to let 6A put something on, as long as he can get us some big publicity in the *Advertiser*?'

'Yes! Because it wouldn't be much good without it,' replied Tim realistically.

'Hey, this sounds good,' commented Ben.

'There'd be no need to send notes out to parents again, Ludo!' said Amy excitedly. 'Of course they're fed up with the Lifeboat Appeal – but they wouldn't need to come! If we organize something and then Mr Gage gets us a big splash in the paper, lots of people from outside'd come along.'

'How about a Grand Jumble Sale?' suggested Ludo. 'Everybody likes those.' He made a quick jotting in the club notebook. 'If we got eighty people along to school they'd only have to spend £1.25 each and there's our £100!'

'Look, I've got it,' said Mini, clapping her hands. 'We'd need a fortnight to collect

21

jumble and everything, if it's going to be a Jumble Sale. If we hold it two weeks on Saturday, that's only two days before the Appeal closes. The paper could say it's a desperate race against time, two days to go, £100 must be raised, that sort of stuff, like a proper news story.'

'It'd be true,' Tim protested. 'It *would* be a proper news story, wouldn't it? I bet Gagey could get the editor to put it in.'

'And a photograph?' suggested Amy. 'One of those lovely old photographs of the Jugmouth lifeboat long ago. That would really catch people's eye.'

'Brill!' said the others.

It had been one of the most productive meetings ever for Handles & Spouts.

Mr Gage was extremely pleased with the whole idea. He suggested to Hands that they form a committee. Dom, Kate and Emily all volunteered; Marcus was forced on to the committee by his mother, who was a Parent Governor and didn't like to see him left out of anything.

As for the *Advertiser*, on which the success of the whole thing hinged, it was just as Hands had hoped: no problem. Mr Gage wrote up the story himself, organized the photograph and the editor readily agreed

to run it, together with a paid advertisement.
The picture of the Jugmouth lifeboat and its
crew in 1927 was so interesting, he said, he'd
be splashing the lot all over the front page.

No wonder their teacher was in a fury.

While Mr Gage was phoning, they all
studied the front page in stunned silence.
The headline said:

JUGMINSTER'S VERY OWN NATIONAL CHAMPION – EMPRESS CLEOPATRA

Beneath the headline was a very large
photograph of the rabbit. It was a close-up
portrait of her, fluffy and sweet, but rather
stupid-looking. The story underneath the
photograph began:

Empress Cleopatra is the tops. She
is a beautiful golden angora rabbit,
owned by Mrs Betty Hopp-Daniels of
Greenacre House, River Lane,
Jugminster. And this week Cleopatra
came top of her class at the All-
England Rabbit Breeders' Show in
London, winning for her proud owner
a coveted Silver Bunny award . . .

There were two smaller photographs below. One showing Mrs Hopp-Daniels shaking hands with someone and receiving the Silver Bunny award; another of her holding Cleopatra and simpering.

Everything else had been pushed off the front page.

'Why would the editor drop our story for this one?' asked Tim crossly, finding his voice at last.

'Maybe he decided it was bigger news,' said Marcus annoyingly.

Ben glowered at Marcus. He was running

a hand through his dark hair, trying to remember something about Mrs Hopp-Daniels. They all knew the name, of course. In fact, she lived almost opposite JVJ. Her big house, Greenacre, was on the corner of River Lane and Bridge Street. Her husband was supposed to have left her pots of money when he died and all his business interests as well . . .

'But why didn't the editor put our story on one of the inside pages, then?' asked Amy, almost in tears.

'And what about our paid advert?' demanded Mini. She'd already been through the paper, page by page. She riffled through it again, just to make sure. 'There was going to be a paid advert!'

'Oh no,' groaned Dom, looking down the Events column. 'The Rotary Club's having a jumble sale tomorrow – and so are the Scouts. Both at two o'clock, like us!'

'Stop it, Dom. I can't stand it!' said Emily in despair.

'Wait a minute, I've got it,' said Ben suddenly. All this time he'd been trying to think of a sensible answer to Tim's question. Ben's family had always lived in Jugminster and he knew a lot about the town. 'He started the *Advertiser*! Mr Hopp-Daniels. He must have left it to her when he died. I bet she owns it! Mrs Hopp-Daniels. And she wanted to show off her flipping rabbit!'

'Quite right, Ben,' said a voice behind them.

Mr Gage had come back into the hall, looking pale.

'I'm afraid she went round to the printer last night and made him discard the front page, in favour of her rabbit story. The first the editor knew about it was when the copies came up this afternoon. He's been trying to ring me at home.'

'What a horrible woman!' exclaimed Tim.

'I'm pleased it wasn't your friend's fault, sir,' said Amy kindly. 'That's a relief.'

'OK, twins, never mind the post-mortem,' replied Mr Gage briskly. 'All that matters now is that we try to rescue the situation – and fast!' He looked around at the anxious faces; took command. 'Let's get the stalls finished as quickly as we can, then we'll write out some notices to pin up. Just handbill size. We'll rush them round town in my car. I can get four of you in my car. And there's *one* bit of good news –'

'What's that?' they all asked eagerly. They were beginning to cheer up, just a bit.

'The *Advertiser*'s passed our news story on to local radio. Seeing the editor can't use it himself! He's dictated my piece over the phone to them – word for word. They've promised to use it on *News Round-Up* tonight. So that's a start!'

They all cheered. 'That's really great!' exclaimed Tim.

'It's a shame about the old photograph of course,' sighed the teacher. 'That really added interest.'

'Can't we think of something else?' suggested Amy. 'Something else that's special? It could go on the handbills and be put out on the radio tonight!'

'Like what?' scoffed Kate Roberts.

'A *Star Attraction*, that's what we want!' said Mini. 'Some famous person!'

'That's right.' Ludo nodded his head. He seemed to be taking the idea seriously. 'We need somebody who'll make everybody want to come to *our* Jumble Sale and not the other two. Especially as we're out on the edge of the town and the other two are bang in the middle.'

'Oh, Ludo, don't be depressing,' protested Emily.

'He's not being depressing, he's trying to

think of something!' retorted Mini. She knew that look of Ludo's.

'I think we should stop chattering and get back to work,' said Mr Gage kindly. 'The hall's not even ready yet and we've still got the handbills to write. Come on, Marcus, let's get this last table up, shall we?'

Hands got the second-hand bookstall finished in double-quick time, while wondering if they knew any famous people. They racked their brains, without success. They *didn't* know any. But Ludo was silent and deep in thought. Suddenly he snapped his fingers.

'Got it!' he said. 'Star Attraction!'

'Who?' asked Ben.

'Not a famous person. A famous rabbit!' said Ludo. 'Maybe she'd lend it!'

'Empress Cleopatra!' gasped Mini. 'Oh, Lu, that's clever.'

Trust Ludo to come up with some lateral thinking.

'You're right, Ludo!' exclaimed Amy. 'The power of publicity. Everybody in town'll be dying to see Cleo by tomorrow. As a matter of fact —' Amy looked rather shamefaced about it — 'I'd like to see Cleo myself. She must be quite something.'

Ben just sniffed, but Tim was enthusiastic.

'D'you think she *would* lend it? She jolly well should, when she's messed up all our publicity. It's the least she could do! Let's go and see what Gagey says!'

Their teacher just smiled at them wryly.

'Run across and speak to her, if you want to,' he said. 'But I don't fancy your chances. And don't be long! I want to get thirty handbills written. That's three each!'

'Maybe we'll be putting the Empress on them,' said Amy hopefully, as the five friends left the school hall.

chapter 3

The Magic Begins

As they hurried up the long front drive of Greenacre House, the Handles decided it would be against their principles to be friendly towards Mrs Hopp-Daniels. Ben and Tim felt particularly strongly about that. So it was agreed that Spouts should do the talking.

It hardly mattered, in fact, who asked her. Because Mrs Hopp-Daniels refused them anyway.

She was giving a tea-party for her grandchildren tomorrow afternoon, she explained. Cleopatra would be the guest of honour. There was a magician coming as well. Besides, being a national champion, the rabbit *was* rather precious. However, she was flattered by their interest and insisted they come round the back to have a peep at Cleopatra there and then, as a special treat.

'So the paper's out already?' she beamed, as she shepherded them along the gravel drive, which continued round to the back of the house.

'It certainly is!' replied Mini brightly, while the boys glowered.

The rabbit had palatial quarters on the back lawn. It could come and go as it pleased. Its open-fronted hutch led on to its very own lush piece of lawn, replete with clover and dandelion stalks, enclosed all the way round by wire mesh. This mesh fencing looked a bit holey in places.

'I like to be able to see her from my kitchens,' explained Mrs Hopp-Daniels. 'She nibbles her way out sometimes, though she never goes far.'

While the boys stayed on the back drive, keeping their distance and looking sulky, she opened the gate of the rabbit run, pulled out Empress Cleopatra and handed her to Amy.

'You can hold her if you like.'

Amy cradled the huge golden bundle of softest angora.

'She's lovely!' she exclaimed, stroking the

31

lustrous, superfine hair. 'I've got a jumper made of golden angora. Just like this! Do you sell her wool sometimes?'

'No, never. She's a show rabbit. She's perfectly spoilt. She doesn't have to earn her keep.' She gazed at the rabbit dotingly. 'Do you, Clee-Clee? You don't have to sell your wool, do you, my precious?'

As Mini joined in the general patting and stroking, the boys kicked at the gravel on the drive, impatient to be off. These gardens at the back of Greenacre House were beautiful, Ludo noticed. The same stream that ran between his and Ben's houses and the Knoll House flowed through them. But here it was no longer wild and reedy-looking; it was spanned by a pretty little wrought-iron bridge and there were ornamental shrubs along the banks.

Tim noticed, as Mrs Hopp-Daniels took her rabbit back from Amy, how rather alike they looked – plump and glossy and full of themselves.

Ben just scowled.

'What a waste of time!' he whispered. 'I knew it would be.'

'Useless,' agreed Tim. 'And I bet she was just making that up about having a children's party and a magician coming and stuff –'

He broke off as an old van rolled quietly past them and pulled up alongside Empress Cleopatra's run. It was a white van, rusted in places. Painted on the side, in faded gold lettering, were the words:

MR AMAZING
The World's Greatest Magician

Ludo grinned. 'Looks like it's true, Timmo.'

A man climbed out of the van and stretched. He gazed all around him, taking in his surroundings. He noted that Greenacre was a splendid house, in fine grounds, and looked gratified.

His clothes were shabby. His shoes were worn out, the soles coming away from the uppers. He obviously never had his hair cut: his shock of grey curls came right to his shoulders. He wore an old straw boater on top of his head, with a frayed silver-and-red ribbon around the brim. He was obviously quite old; an old, down-at-heel magician. But his blue, popping eyes had a certain intensity about them.

Amy and Mini turned round and stared at him.

34

For Amy, straight away, Mr Amazing had a kind of magical aura of his own. Who was he? Was his name really Mr Amazing? Where did he come from? For he cut a strange figure, standing there by his rusted van in the pale sunshine, against the expensive backdrop of Greenacre House.

Mrs Hopp-Daniels had just put Cleopatra back in the run and closed its little gate. Now she straightened up and turned round, too.

'Can I help you?' she asked in surprise, an expression of slight distaste crossing her face.

He walked forward and extended his hand, which she pretended not to notice. He had magician's hands – long-fingered, sinewy, supple.

'Mr Amazing. You booked in the summer. I would like to rest before dinner. My room is ready?'

A red flush started to creep up the woman's cheeks.

'I have come a long way, madam. My agent explained to you that I'd require accommodation? I need time to get to know my surroundings, in peace and contemplation. I need to know and under-stand Jugminster. I shall be quite happy with steak or chicken. I am not a vegetarian.'

With a faintly horrified expression, Mrs Hopp-Daniels pushed straight past him and headed towards the back entrance of the house.

'Wait just there!' she babbled. 'Stay right where you are. There's been a mix-up. I meant to write a letter –'

'Letter, madam?'

But the back door slammed.

'Come on,' whispered Ben, shifting from one foot to the other. 'We'd better get going! We promised Gagey we wouldn't be long!'

But Amy couldn't take her eyes off Mr Amazing. She walked right up to him.

'Have you ever been on TV?' she asked shyly. Shabby and seedy-looking he might be, but there was something special about him. He looked like a *real* magician. Those eyes – they sort of hypnotized you.

He bowed.

'Never,' he said. 'Proper magic can happen only in the flesh-and-blood world. There must be a special telepathy between the magician and those who believe in him. It is not simply a spectacle to be gawped at. All must play their part! I limit myself solely to personal appearances. And those only when the signs are right. The aspect between Mars and Saturn is remarkable this weekend. The energy fields are very strong –'

He broke off.

Mrs Hopp-Daniels was coming out of the house, waving something. She'd been hurriedly writing a cheque.

Amy backed away and stood with the others as the woman came heaving up. She placed the cheque in Mr Amazing's hand.

'An oversight, I'm afraid,' she said in a fluttery way. 'Do take this. Compensation. I forgot to write to your agent and cancel. You see,' she blathered, not even noticing his hurt expression, 'the Great Mystico's coming tomorrow! I've booked him. I'm so sorry. I met him at Lady Stibley's children's party last month. I booked him on the spot. Quite, quite brilliant! Here, the cheque, do take it. I insist.'

Impassively, Mr Amazing took the cheque. He folded it over and over, then over and over again. It got tinier and tinier, smaller than a postage stamp, until it seemed to disappear altogether. And at that moment . . .

He pointed up to the sky.

'Destroy!' he cried, as they all looked up.

And, quite out of nowhere it seemed, the

cheque appeared in tiny pieces all over the woman's hair, just like confetti.

'Hey, *that* was good!' whispered Ben.

Amy just gasped in amazement.

'*No one* is as brilliant as Mr Amazing!' he informed Mrs Hopp-Daniels witheringly, as she tried to pick the tiny fragments of cheque out of her hair. 'Keep your money, madam. You have just insulted the world's greatest magician. I don't want your charity. You are a stupid, ignorant woman.'

He climbed back into his van and switched on the engine.

'What a rude man!' said Mrs Hopp-Daniels with a shrug. She glared at Handles & Spouts. 'Off you go, then. You've seen Cleopatra now!'

As she stomped off into her house again, Tim said, 'What a rude *woman*, more like it.'

They walked over to the van; the driver's window was down. Mr Amazing was looking into the wing mirror and preparing to back the vehicle and turn.

'Don't take any notice of her, sir,' said Tim sympathetically. 'She's horrible.'

It was then that Amy got completely carried away. Her heart was thumping. They mustn't let Mr Amazing go. This was fate, wasn't it? What was that he'd said about the planets being in the right place and the strong energy fields?

'I wish you could work some magic for *us*!' she blurted out. 'We wanted her to lend us her rabbit, so we'd have a Star Attraction tomorrow. But she can't lend it.'

Mr Amazing switched off the engine and listened with interest. 'Star Attraction?' he said.

'Our Grand Jumble Sale's going to be a flop!' grumbled Tim. 'It's all because of her rabbit winning something!'

'It pinched all our publicity,' explained Ben.

'*I* shall be your Star Attraction,' stated Mr Amazing. He said it quite suddenly.

'But we can't afford to pay you, sir,' protested Ben. 'We haven't got any money. I mean, we'd like to book you up but –'

'Money?' said Mr Amazing disdainfully. 'Not necessary.'

He looked at Amy and smiled a wonderful smile.

'So you are in difficulty? How very fortunate, the good aspect between Mars and Saturn. How lucky we have met. Not for nothing am I known as the world's greatest magician.'

Amy stared into his popping blue eyes, quite mesmerized.

Behind her back the other four secretly exchanged glances, raised questioning eyebrows. But they didn't have to think about it very long.

Mr Amazing mightn't look much, but he was better than nothing. That trick with the cheque had been pretty impressive.

Mini gave a thumbs-up signal, eyes shining.

The boys exchanged nods and returned Mini's signal.

At least this would be better than returning to school empty-handed.

And Mr Amazing was saying to Amy, 'Yes, I shall be the star you seek. I will magic the crowds along. They will come! And I, Mr Amazing, shall amaze them. How lucky our meeting. You see, already the magic has started.'

That was Amy's opinion, too.

Tim Cools Off

*T*hey directed the van straight across to JVJ, all running along beside it. Amy felt thrilled. Surely Mr Gage would see how brilliant this was! They'd raise the £100 for the Lifeboat Appeal now. She was convinced of that. She had total faith in Mr Amazing.

The van crawled through the school gates, then drew up in the playground, right outside the school hall.

Mr Gage and the others peered through the windows and saw the words *The World's Greatest Magician* on the side of the van. The next moment, Hands were propelling the driver towards the hall. He was a strange, shock-haired, pop-eyed-looking character.

'What's going on?' exclaimed Mr Gage.

'They were supposed to find out about

the rabbit,' giggled Kate. She looked excited. 'He's not a rabbit.'

'He's a magician!' realized Emily.

'Looks more like a tramp to me,' said Marcus.

Dom was absorbed in writing a handbill. He was leaning over a table near the door, all his felt-tips spread out in front of him. He looked up in surprise as Mr Amazing came in and swept past his table.

The magician, who seemed wrapped in his own thoughts, strode down the hall and made straight for the stage. While they all watched, he ran up the steps and on to the stage. He gazed at the banner that 6A had made in their art lesson.

JUGMOUTH LIFEBOAT APPEAL – LAST CHANCE

As featured in the local press

PLEASE HELP US TO HELP THEM!

Then he raised his arms aloft and twirled round, exclaiming, 'Yes, I like the atmosphere. The atmosphere is right.'

He smiled and called across to Mr Gage, 'An excellent stage, sir. I can perform magic here. Magic undreamed of!'

He started to walk backwards and forwards across the stage, muttering to himself.

'He's offered to come *free* tomorrow,' Amy whispered to the open-mouthed teacher. She explained how they'd met him. 'He says he can magic the crowds along and put everything right for us. Please say yes, sir!' she begged.

Mr Gage looked a bit doubtful. But then Mr Amazing descended lightly from the stage and pointed a tapering finger at Dom, who'd now joined the others.

'Come here, my son. You have lost something?'

Dom walked towards him, looking puzzled.

'Lost something?' he asked. 'Don't think so, sir. Like what?'

Mr Amazing laughed. He threw his hand up and seemed to catch something as it fell out of the air. It was a felt-tipped pen. Then he plucked a second one out of the air and a third from behind Dom's left ear. He handed all three felt-tips over.

'Yours, I believe?'

Dom took them, with a gasp. They were his felt-tips all right. His name was on them. But surely he'd left them on the table, at

the other end of the hall! Everyone cheered and, as she caught Mr Gage's eye, Amy gave a little shiver of excitement. Their teacher was smiling.

'OK!' he said. 'Splendid.'

He stepped forward to shake the magician by the hand. He was scruffy, he decided, but well-meaning. And he knew his stuff! They were hardly in a position to look a gift-horse in the mouth. Talking of which, the poor chap's false teeth were dreadful. Where had he had *those* made?

'We'll be very honoured to have you

45

here tomorrow,' said Mr Gage. 'It's very generous of you, I must say.'

Mr Amazing warmly returned the handshake.

'Nothing will give me greater satisfaction,' he said.

While Mr Gage went off to phone the local radio station, the rest of them set to work on the handbills, adding their special announcement, of course:

STAR ATTRACTION
MR AMAZING – World's Greatest Magician

The great man wandered around, looking over their shoulders from time to time and nodding sagely. When Mr Gage returned and told him that the radio announcement was all fixed, he smiled and went up on stage again. He lingered there for some time, exploring, humming softly to himself. In spite of his long journey, and having lost his meal and bed for the night at Greenacre House, he seemed in no hurry to leave and make new arrangements.

At six o'clock, when everything was done and the hall locked up, he stood in the playground by his van, talking to Mr Gage.

Marcus, Dom, Kate and Emily climbed into Mr Gage's car, with their notices. They were going to make a quick dash round the centre of town with them. Ben and Ludo were going to do the Waterfront, on foot. They were sure that Dolly's and the fish-and-chip shop would each take one for a start.

The twins and Mini decided that they'd better cover Back Lane, River Lane and the River Arms. Their teacher called them over.

'Mr Amazing's van is at your disposal,' Gagey said. He was smiling, so they knew that everything was all right and their teacher approved. 'He has asked my permission to give you a lift, if you need one. It's very kind of him.'

'Thanks!' said Tim gratefully. 'That'll be good. Then we can get home and have some supper. It's beef stew and dumplings tonight. I'm starving.'

'Are you sure you can spare the time?' asked Amy anxiously, noticing that Mr Amazing's mouth appeared to be watering. 'I mean, you haven't got yourself fixed up yet.'

'But if we go down to the River Arms, you could book in there!' said Mini helpfully; also worried at the thought of the lift slipping away. 'It's supposed to be really good.'

'Mini's right,' said Mr Gage. He shook hands with Mr Amazing once more. 'The River Arms is *very* good and the rooms are quite cheap. I can certainly recommend it. Till tomorrow, then. Many thanks!'

And they all went their separate ways.

But Mr Amazing didn't show the least interest in booking into the River Arms. When they reached the old inn, he just sat in the car-park while his three young friends hurried off with the handbill. They'd managed to place all the rest, so this was the last call, though Mini was saving one for her garden gate.

The landlord knew Mr Dalladay well and was very helpful. He promised to put their notice up in his biggest bar, the Boatmen's.

'I am not a rich man,' Mr Amazing explained, as he drove them home afterwards. 'The River Arms, delightful inn though it is, is quite beyond my means.'

There was an uncomfortable silence in the van as it cruised along Back Lane.

They dropped Mini off outside number

27, just opposite the Knoll House. They watched her pin the handbill on her front gate before waving their goodbyes. Then Mr Amazing scrunched into the Knoll House's pot-holed drive and drove the twins round the back to their kitchen door. Tim and Amy sat silently in the van for a little while, thinking hard.

Surely, thought Amy, for Mr Amazing all things were possible?

'Couldn't you magic your cheque back together again?' she asked him tentatively.

He gazed at her, smiled, then shook his head.

'A real magician can perform magic only for other people,' he explained. 'For *others* but not for himself! Have you never realized that fact before?'

Amy considered it carefully.

'I get you,' she said.

'But what'll you do then?' asked Tim, practical as usual.

'Buy a large bag of chips and spend the night in the back of the van somewhere,' Mr Amazing replied with dignity. 'I have a sleeping-bag.'

'Oh,' said Amy.

The big, oak kitchen door squeaked open and Mrs Dalladay appeared with their little brother struggling in her arms. Harry had been screeching to come outside.

'See, Harry?' said Mum. 'It's *not* Daddy's car. He's not back yet. It's Amy and Tim. Mr Gage must have given them a lift.'

'Mamie and Timmy!' exclaimed the little boy eagerly, as they clambered out of the van.

'About time, you two!' said Mum. 'Your supper's waiting. Everything ready for tomorrow? Oh –'

She broke off in surprise as the odd-looking figure emerged with the shock of grey hair and strange popping eyes. For the first time, she took in the words on the side of the van: *MR AMAZING – The World's Greatest Magician*.

'We've found a magician for tomorrow, Mum!' said Tim.

'Yes, so I see,' replied Mrs Dalladay. 'How – how nice.'

'Delicious!' announced Mr Amazing, sniffing the air deeply. 'What can you be cooking, madam?' The aroma came at him from the open back door in great wafts. The aroma of beef stewed in herbs and red wine. 'What a wonderful smell.'

'Mr Amazing's going to make sure everything comes right for us tomorrow,

Mum,' explained Amy, propelling him forward. 'He's going to magic along the crowds for us.'

'Free!' said Tim.

'Mr Gage's ever so pleased we found him,' added Amy quickly. Anyone would think he was a scarecrow or something, the way Mum was looking him up and down.

But Mrs Dalladay was merely deciding that he looked badly in need of a square meal. Now, she gave him a smile; nervous but welcoming.

'You must stay to supper,' she said. 'Could you manage some food?'

'Bajic!' shouted Harry excitedly.

'Just a little something, perhaps,' murmured Mr Amazing.

As they all trooped into the warm kitchen, Amy and Tim both felt relieved: for his sake. Good old Mum.

But by cocoa-time Tim's mood had changed somewhat. He was cooling off the whole idea of Mr Amazing. Amy was very disappointed in Tim. She was surprised at his lack of faith.

chapter 5

A Case Beckons

*T*he twins sipped their cocoa up in Tim's bedroom, in pyjamas and dressing-gowns. It was nearly time for *News Round-Up* on local radio. It always came on at nine o'clock, straight after *Happy Hour*. Amy snuggled into her bean-bag, which she'd dragged across from her room. Her own radio was down at HQ.

'Well, this is it,' said Tim nervously, as he tuned in his radio. He was sitting cross-legged on the floor. 'I hope it's going to be all right. They'd better give Mr Amazing a really big splurge. They'd better make him sound brilliant!'

'Oh do stop fussing, Tim,' said Amy. *Happy Hour* was just signing off with some pop music and it was the week's number one. She tapped her left foot in time to it. 'He'll magic the crowds along anyway, whatever they say about him. He promised. He told us at supper that *whatever* happens, we'll get our £100! If you don't *believe* in magic, Tim, nothing magic ever *happens* to you.'

'H'm,' said Tim with a frown. 'He couldn't even magic himself some food and a bed for the night.'

'That's different,' retorted Amy. 'He can't do magic for himself, only for other people. You haven't listened to a thing he's said!'

'So I presume that's why we've had to lend him the caravan!' said Tim indignantly. 'Fancy a magician having nowhere to sleep for the night. You know all our secret stuff's in there. *Nobody's* allowed in there!'

During supper, Mr Amazing had held Harry spellbound – and Amy, too! He'd made Harry's teddy bear talk and sugar lumps appear in its paw. But afterwards he'd rather slumped, with tiredness, and said he needed peace and quiet to prepare himself for tomorrow. To the twin's surprise, Mum had insisted they lend him the caravan for the night. She wouldn't hear of him going off to sleep in the van somewhere!

Privately very put out by this, Tim had offered to give up his own bedroom. But Mum said *no*, and Mr Amazing said the caravan would suit him perfectly. He'd gone straight outside, locked up the van with his precious suitcases inside, then toddled off down the garden, with torch and sleeping-bag.

'To sleep, perchance to dream!' he'd said, giving Amy an extra-special smile. 'Tomorrow I shall do wondrous things.'

'It's a shame about HQ,' conceded Amy, now. 'But it's all in a good cause. And he

54

promised to leave it spick and span, didn't he?'

He'd said: *Tomorrow, when I have gone away for ever, you will not find the smallest sign that Mr Amazing was in your midst.* It had sent a little shiver down Amy's spine. It made him seem really mysterious somehow. A figure in a dream.

'Huh,' said Tim. He was feeling cross and on edge.

It wasn't just the matter of Club HQ being taken over, unsettling though that was. There was something else. But there was no point in discussing it with Amy. At the moment she was acting a bit as though she'd been hypnotized!

Tim had overheard Dad and Mum talking in the kitchen. It was while Amy was upstairs, reading Harry his bedtime story.

Mr Amazing had disappeared down to the caravan for the night and Dad had just got in. He'd been sorting out someone's desk-top system for them and it had taken ages. He was tired and hungry and his voice had sounded irritable.

'Well, he might be half-starved, but did he have to magic my supper away? No . . . look . . . come and have a look in the pot yourself . . . What d'you mean, darling, you didn't see him take a second helping? He must have done!'

Tim couldn't catch what Mum said. Her voice was all low and soft and soothing. But then he heard Dad's again –

'. . . complete waste of time! The rugby's on TV tomorrow afternoon. Can't see many people dragging themselves out to watch a magic show!'

With sinking heart, Tim had crept away. Rugby on TV. That was *all* they needed. No wonder he felt on edge.

The pop song had finished and *Happy Hour* was fading out. Amy started to say something but Tim put his fingers to his lips. *News Round-Up* was beginning. They were singing the special jingle – *All the local news . . . tra-la . . . everything to choose . . . tra-la . . .* Round-Up*!*

Tim folded his arms and stared at the radio and listened carefully. He was clenching and unclenching his knuckles, to relieve the tension.

It's nine o'clock exactly *and all the Jug Valley news is coming up right now*, said a breezy voice. *Lots to do and see in the Valley tomorrow. And a very big story's broken this evening in*

Jugminster. It's exclusive to Round-Up, *so stay tuned, folks . . .*

Amy clapped her hands triumphantly as the jingle played again: *All the local news . . . tra-la . . .*

'See!' she told Tim. 'Mr Amazing's going to get his big splurge!'

'Ssh!' said Tim. He suddenly looked hopeful. 'I want to hear!'

The announcer came breezing back over the airwaves.

Right, folks. As I said, a big, big *story in Jugminster, so mind you stay tuned. But first a quick round-up of some of the really great events that are taking place all round the valley tomorrow.*

He rattled through a list of events along the Jug Valley, all planned for Saturday. Bingos, discos, exhibitions, jumble sales. Including one at –

. . . Jug Valley Juniors! It's their last chance to meet their target for the Jugmouth Lifeboat Appeal. Yes, folks, their very last chance. And they're throwing in a magic show for free. Last but not least, don't forget the art exhibition in Jugminster Library – it closes tomorrow. And now we come to our big story . . .

'Oh,' said Amy. 'Is that all we get?'

Tim's spirits crashed into his boots. So

they *weren't* the big story, after all! And
then, he could hardly believe his ears –

    *. . . There's a very naughty rabbit gone
walkabout in Jugminster, somewhere in River
Lane. No ordinary bunny, I can tell you, but our
famous local champ, Empress Cleopatra. She's a
big bundle of fun with long gold fur and she's
escaped from her run tonight – yes, escaped!
The owner's rung in and she's had to call the
search off overnight. But she's offering a big,* big
*reward to the lucky finder. Pencil and paper ready?
Here are all the details . . . Fancy a picture of
Empress in a gilt frame . . .?*

    Click!

'Oh, I wanted to hear about Cleo!'
protested Amy, as Tim switched off his
radio in disgust.

'I don't believe it!' he fumed. 'She's done
it again! She's pinched all our publicity
again just because her stupid rabbit's
got out.' He buried his face in his hands,
in despair. 'They say that lightning
can't strike in the same place twice.
Well, it just has. Of all the rotten, horrible
luck . . .'

Amy tried to calm him down.

'I know, it's awful, but if you ask me
we're just not *meant* to have any big
publicity, Tim.' She stared at the window

58

panes. Huge raindrops were suddenly splashing against them. All their handbills! They'd be all soggy and smudged by the morning! 'Maybe we're not even meant to have any small publicity. D'you know what I think, Tim?'

She looked at her brother brightly.

'What?' he grunted.

'I think that's why Mr Amazing's been sort of sent to us. To put everything right. It's fate! It's all part of the magic.'

'Don't be corny, Amy,' he said. He felt hatred stirring within him for Mrs Hopp-Daniels. 'We've had it now! Nobody's going to come. He's not really world-famous. They didn't even bother to say his name on the radio! He'll do his show in front of an empty hall.'

'He's never said he's world-*famous* – just the world's greatest!'

But Tim got to his feet and walked over to the window. He looked out into the night and watched the rain coming down.

'I know what *you* think, Amy. Now I'll tell you what *I* think. We're going to look stupid at JVJ on Monday! We've boasted we're going to raise that £100. Mort even announced the news in assembly. 6A have saved the day, he said. Well, we're *not*. And we *haven't*. What a hope!'

'You can think what you like,' said Amy, on her dignity at being called corny. She backed out of the room, dragging her bean-bag with her. 'But I think you're *wrong*! Talk about looking on the black side! I'm really tired, Tim. It's Gym Club in the morning. I'm going to bed.'

Moments later, her bedroom door slammed shut.

When Mini phoned through, ten minutes later, Amy was already fast asleep. So Tim took the call instead.

'Wasn't that a rip-off!' exclaimed Mini. She seemed to be making little sounds in her throat. Tim wondered for a moment if she was trying not to cry. 'And you should see the notice on my gate. It's practically washed away. I expect they all are!'

Tim suddenly realized that she was giggling slightly, in excitement.

'Looks like fate, doesn't it, Tim?' she said cheerfully.

'Oh no,' groaned Tim. 'Not you as well. That's what Amy said.'

'What's the matter with *you*?' asked Mini.

'You're usually all excited when a case beckons.'

'Case?'

'Yes. I've just phoned Lu. Ben's round at his house. They listened to the radio together. They both think my idea's fantastic, Tim. If we get up early, we can find Cleo before anyone else does. Mrs Hopp-Daniels said it never goes far. We're detectives, aren't we? Don't you realize, Tim, your stream goes right through Greenacre. Right through the grounds! It'll be *easy* –'

'Find her rabbit for her?' began Tim, feeling indignant and trying to get a word in edgeways. But a Spout in full flow wasn't easily stanched –

'– and Ben says he'll bring Jax! He says Jax is a fantastic rabbiter – he can scent one a mile off. He'll pick up Cleopatra's trail for us. Oh, Tim, don't you think this just *has* to be fate? We've as good as made that £100 reward already! We won't accept it for ourselves, of course,' added Mini quickly. 'We'll make her give it to JVJ's Lifeboat Appeal.' The giggles bubbled out properly now. 'Poetic justice. That's what Lu calls it!'

Tim's scalp prickled slightly.

£100! Just for a rabbit?

He hadn't believed that stuff on the radio about a big, *big* reward. They always said everything was either *big* or *wonderful*, like the free poster he'd sent off for once, which turned out to be small and grotty. He hadn't been interested in Mrs Hopp-Daniels' reward, especially as it sounded as if it was going to be just the photo of her rabbit! He'd switched the radio off . . .

£100!

'Anything wrong?' Mini was asking.

'No fear!' said Tim quickly. *What an ace case for Hands,* he thought. *Good old Mini!*

He rapped out instructions for the morning and Mini said she'd pass them on to Ludo and Ben.

Tim was just turning away from the phone, feeling excited, when it rang again. This time it was Marcus King.

It was a slightly panicky phone call; he was wishing heartily that his mother hadn't got him into things.

'You lot call yourself detectives, don't you? You live near Mrs What's-it's place. Why don't you get up early and find her rabbit for her?'

'D'you think we haven't thought of that?' replied Tim stiffly. 'It's all in hand.'

'Good!' said Marcus. 'No hope of raising

£100 any other way! Dad says it's the rugby on TV. If you ask me, we're all going to look fools and that Mr Amazing you've found is going to look the biggest fool of the lot.'

'He's a very *good* magician,' replied Tim loyally. Behind him, the front door clicked open. It was Mr Dalladay, returning from the pub. 'So nobody's interested in *your* opinion. It's not his fault if there's stuff on TV! And, anyway, if you're so clever, why didn't *you* go out and find a Star Attraction for free, like we did!'

Tim slammed the phone down and poked his tongue out at it.

His father came up and placed a hand on his shoulder. It was rather a wet hand because he'd just walked back from the River Arms in the rain. He pulled an envelope out of his pocket. Written on it were the words JUGMOUTH LIFEBOAT APPEAL.

'Liked the notice, Tim. Saw it in the bar. Really eye-catching. Some of the lads had a whip-round. There's six pounds in this envelope. I'll give it to Mummy to look after.'

'Six pounds!' exclaimed Tim, turning round. He smiled at his father. 'Thanks, Dad!'

'Real shame it's the big match
tomorrow,' said Dad. 'And Mummy says
there are two other jumble sales *and* the
free sheet's let you down. What a stinker.
Life's like that, full of ups and downs. You
just have to learn to come up smiling!'

'Yes, Dad.'

Tim turned and ran upstairs. He was
smiling already.

With Ben's dog Jax to help them, they
were going to be out on the trail early,
before the rest of the town was awake.

They'd find Cleopatra and take her back

to her owner. Mrs Hopp-Daniels would still be having her breakfast. Or maybe she'd be just getting up.

They'd hand over the rabbit and collect that cheque for £100 from her. They'd tell her they wanted it made out to the JVJ Lifeboat Appeal account.

With knobs on.

chapter 6

Locked Out of HQ!

*U*nfortunately, Tim hadn't bothered to mention to Mini that their HQ had been taken over. So Ben and Ludo didn't know either.

They'd decided to get to the caravan early and have a working breakfast. They kept a large-scale map of Jugminster in HQ. They knew which way the stream went to reach Mrs Hopp-Daniels's grounds. But they had a feeling it went underground before it reached Bridge Street. They might have to work out an approach from a different direction. The map would be useful.

The idea was to get into the grounds secretly, before Mrs Hopp-Daniels was awake. Jax would need to get a good sniff round Cleopatra's run, in order to pick up the trail. Before the *rest* of the town was awake, too! The entire area would be swarming with bounty-hunters later on – but Hands were going to beat them to it!

Ben slipped out of his patio door at first light, with Jax on the lead. Ludo was waiting for him in the back garden, with a packet of cereal and a carton of milk.

'Sugar puffs. Good!' whispered Ben.

'Right. Let's go,' said Ludo.

The Johnsons and the Browns lived in adjoining semis on the small housing estate behind the Knoll House. Their gardens ran down to the Dalladays' stream. The caravan was parked on the bank just opposite. They'd made a foot-bridge across the stream a long time ago, out of wooden planks. In the old days they just used it as a short cut to school, always calling for Tim on the way. But now, of course, they used it to get to HQ as well.

It was great, the way they could glimpse HQ from their bedroom windows: chinks of pale yellow amongst drooping willow branches, beyond the hawthorn and brambles. It was well camouflaged.

They pushed through the bushes at the bottom of Ben's garden now. Jax was

straining on the leash to get to the foot-
bridge and cross over the stream. He liked
it in the Dalladays' orchard.

'He can practise rabbit-hunting while
we're having breakfast,' said Ben with a
grin. 'I'll let him off the lead for a while.'

'Hey, he won't try and eat Cleopatra,
will he?' asked Ludo in alarm. 'When he
finds her?'

''Course not,' said Ben. 'He'll be quite
happy when I give him some fudge. It'll be
his reward. Look.'

Ben pulled a large Cellophane bag from
the pocket of his anorak. It was crammed
full of fudge, cut into cubes. Home-made
fudge was Ben's speciality. It was always
delicious.

'You made that for the sweets stall!'
protested Ludo. 'Better leave some for the
customers!'

Ben glanced up at the leaden sky. The
heavy rain overnight had stopped. But
more was forecast.

'What customers?' he asked.

Ludo nodded. And, making the best of
it, said, 'Let's have a piece then, Ben!'

They crossed the slippy bridge; then
squelched, in their wellington boots,
through the long, wet grass to the caravan.

The fudge was melting deliciously in their mouths. They couldn't wait to get into HQ and set to work on the rabbit case.

'Oi, that's funny – the door's locked!' exclaimed Ben as he rattled the handle.

They never bothered to lock up HQ. It wasn't necessary.

'It can't be –' said Ludo. 'Wait a minute, the curtains are drawn as well –'

Suddenly Jax launched himself at the door of the caravan, growling excitedly. The long, low growl built up to a crescendo: 'GRRR . . . YELP . . . WOOOFFF . . . *WOOOFFF*!'

As Jax scrabbled furiously at the door, Ben struggled to yank him back. At the same time they heard someone moving around inside – and then a man's voice, raised in anger!

'GO AWAY.'

The boys looked at one another in astonishment. Someone was in their HQ. What a cheek! Then they realized it was Mr Amazing.

He was telling them to go away!

Meanwhile, Mini, equally keen to get started, had arrived early at the Knoll House. She stood in the kitchen in old clothes and wellington boots, warming her hands at the big Aga stove. Tim was looking for his boots and anorak, while Amy was finishing her breakfast, in silence.

'Like my plan, Amy?' asked Mini. 'Good?'

'Great,' said Amy nobly. She wasn't going to be critical of a fellow Spout. Besides, it was a relief to see Tim looking cheerful again. Secretly she wondered if Hands would be able to succeed where Mrs Hopp-Daniels had failed.

She still pinned much hope on Mr Amazing.

The £6 collected at the River Arms last night was a magical beginning. When you had *World's Greatest Magician* on your notices, it caught the eye. It was a pity some of them would be washed away by now. Still . . . six pounds. Only another ninety-four to go.

Amy spooned some damson jelly on to her last corner of toast. She'd made it, back in the summer, with Mum's help. They'd had a good crop of damsons this year. Delicious.

She found her wellies in the corner and hauled them on. If they were going to follow the stream, she'd need them. Big, high waders would be better, like Dad wore when he went fishing.

'Yes, it'll be good going to look for Cleo,' she said. 'We ought to give it a try. As long as it doesn't make us late for Gym Club.'

'Gym Club?' asked Tim, raising his eyebrows. He was now pacing up and down the red flag-stoned floor, impatient to go and intercept Ben and Ludo. 'If we miss activities this week, it's just too bad. This case is much too important, Amy. Urgent. We don't want to look stupid on Monday, do we?'

Activities at JVJ on Saturday morning were voluntary. They all liked Gym Club, except for Ludo, who belonged to Chess Club. But they weren't forced to turn up. However –

'We can't miss activities!' protested Amy in alarm.

Mini looked at her best friend in surprise.

'Oh, I'm sure we'll be back,' she said, humouring her. What did activities matter, compared with this? 'Jax'll find old Clee-Clee in no time. As long as nobody else finds her first! Come on, Amy, get a move on. We'll need the map, won't we, Tim? Let's go down to HQ and find it –'

Tim opened the kitchen door and squinted through, looking uneasy.

'Yes. I've thought of that. There's a bit of a problem, Mini. We're going to have to wake Mr Amazing up.'

'Wake *who* up?' asked Mini.

'D'you mean you haven't told anybody, Tim?' asked Amy in horror. She opened the big oak door wide. 'Supposing Ben and Lu go to HQ with Jax? *They*'ll wake Mr Amazing up. They'll give him a fright. You know how tired he was last night! We've got to look after him. He needs peace and quiet. I don't think he ought to be disturbed –'

She broke off. From the bottom of the orchard came the faint sounds of Jax barking and a voice raised in anger.

'Looks like he already has been,' said Mini.

And the three of them raced down to the caravan.

'Sorry to wake you up, sir,' said Tim, tapping on the door of their HQ, 'but we want to ask you something.'

'*Take that dog away!*' shouted the voice within.

Jax was straining on the leash, desperate

72

to get into the caravan. 'Woof!' Tim gave Ben an urgent hand signal which said, *Get him to back off, for goodness' sake, Ben!*

Ben dragged Jax off along the banks of the stream and crouched with him behind some bushes, hanging on tight and giving him a piece of fudge. 'Now shut *up*, boy!' he hissed. 'Be*have*.'

Only then did the caravan door open, just a little bit. 'Well?' asked Mr Amazing, peering out.

'*Leave* it, Tim,' whispered Amy, trying to tug him away. She could see that Mr Amazing was standing in his sleeping-bag, holding it up with his armpits. 'It's not fair!'

But her brother stood his ground.

'Can I just pop in and get something, please?' blurted out Tim. 'It's really urgent. You see, that prize rabbit's escaped and we're going to find it and we need our map –'

'What concern is it of ours if that stupid, ignorant woman has lost her rabbit?' the magician asked witheringly.

'There's £100 reward!' spoke up Ludo. 'We need it for the Lifeboat Appeal!'

Mr Amazing showed not the slightest interest.

'You are wasting your time,' he said calmly. 'Have I not already promised you that I, Mr Amazing, will do wondrous things? Your coffers will be filled to overflowing. You must have faith in me –'

Every time he said it, it sent a little thrill through Amy. But Mini wasn't taking any notice. She was looking brisk.

'Please, sir, can't Tim just pop in and get our map?'

'Begone!' he commanded, with equal briskness. 'This is my inner sanctum. I am preparing to make magic for you. Nobody enters here today. *Nobody!*'

They all backed away nervously. Slowly the door closed in their faces and they heard the catch click.

They were being locked out of their own HQ!

'*Don't* give us the map, then!' exclaimed Tim crossly, then turned on his heel. The others followed him to the bushes, where Ben was waiting with Jax. Amy glanced back over her shoulder, pink-cheeked with embarrassment. Whatever would Mr Amazing think of Tim, saying that?

'We'll just have to manage without it,' grinned Ben.

'Yes, let's get going,' said Tim.

'What do I do with *these*?' asked Ludo, holding up the packet of sugar puffs and the carton of milk.

'Give them to me!' said Amy. She took them from Ludo eagerly. 'I'll catch you up.'

As the Handles dog-handled Jax and headed off downstream, Amy walked back to the caravan and tapped on the door.

Mr Amazing peered through the window, then cautiously half-opened the door again. Amy gazed up at him.

'Please don't take any notice of my brother, sir,' she said. 'He didn't mean to be rude. We do have faith in you – well, I do. I really do.'

The blue, mesmerizing eyes met hers and he smiled gently.

'I know you do, my dear. And you shall not be disappointed.'

Yesterday he'd spoken with confidence. But today, it seemed to Amy, it was more than that – it was absolute certainty.

'We're ever so grateful to you for helping us out,' she said shyly. She held aloft the milk and the box of sugar puffs. She was about to ask him if he'd mind keeping them safe, in the caravan.

'How very kind,' he said, taking them from her. 'My favourite.'

76

'Hurry up, Amy!' yelled Mini, who'd paused to wait for her.

So Amy merely returned his smile, then fled.

chapter 7

The Great Rabbit Hunt

*M*ini and Amy had to run to catch the boys up. They plunged through the bushes, along the stream's bank, then wriggled under the wire fence that separated the Knoll House's garden from Mr Vincent's field.

It was a tiny field, with a few sheep grazing on it. The boys were already half-way across, following the course of the stream. Jax was straining at the leash, setting a cracking pace. He glanced round at the sheep once or twice, but Ben kept a firm grip on him.

'Woof!' said Jax, and Hands were relieved to know there'd be no chance of bumping into Mr Vincent. It was fun being up so early, long before anyone else!

'I just hope we can follow the stream right into her grounds,' Tim said. 'Otherwise we're going to *need* that map.'

'Well, we haven't got it, so let's forget about it,' said Amy firmly.

'Locked out of our own HQ!' he muttered. But he was getting over it. He was beginning to feel excited. This should be interesting.

The great rabbit hunt had begun.

Ahead of them the stream flowed under a line of iron palings – the Back Lane bridge.

'D'you think we'll be able to squeeze through them?' Amy asked Ben.

'Well, Mini might be able to, but I can't,' laughed Ben. 'It's all right. We can go under the road. It means ducking our heads and getting our boots wet, but it's quick and easy.'

Jax led the way under the tiny arch of the bridge, barking eagerly and splashing through the water. Ben ducked his head and followed. He laughed again. He liked this. He loved action! The others followed him through the archway, bending their heads, paddling in the stream. They were passing right under Back Lane; it was dark and dank in here. The stone walls were all slimy as they pressed against them.

'Creepy!' giggled Mini.

They emerged into daylight again. They were on to a much larger field, common land. A line of willows meandered across it into the distance, showing them the course of the stream. They walked along its banks in silence. It was eerie, the early-morning stillness.

The stream was wild and rushy, full of little fish. Half-way across, Amy thought she saw a moorhen bob out of sight. A duck and drake were searching for food, bottoms up. Amy wondered if it was the pair that came up to the back door of the Knoll House sometimes for crusts of bread.

Three-quarters of the way across, a cow got up from its sitting position against a willow, stumblingly.

'That's a bad sign,' said Ludo, as it lumbered out of their way with a brown-eyed stare. 'Cows sitting down mean it's going to rain.'

'Well, it said so on TV, anyway, you nut!' laughed Mini.

'Oh, did it really?' said Amy, disappointed. 'More rain?'

But now Tim was quickening his pace to a run, shading his eyes. The field ran only as far as Bridge Street, which was less than 200 metres ahead.

'What happens to the stream now?' he shouted to Ben over his shoulder. 'That's the big question!'

He was keyed up. They wanted to get into the grounds of Greenacre House and look for Cleopatra before her owner was up and about. They certainly weren't going to risk walking up the front drive. Or asking permission, either. And they knew the stream flowed through the grounds.

Although Greenacre House fronted on to River Lane, its grounds were bounded to the west by a high wall along the far side of Bridge Street. How did the stream get from the common, under Bridge Street (which was quite a wide road) and into Mrs Hopp-Daniels's grounds? Would it be passable, or would they have to make some complicated detour – and without the help of their map?

'I've never noticed it from Bridge Street, Tim!' Ben was saying, tugging at Jax's lead. Jax had slowed down, to look at a cow. 'I've a feeling it goes underground –'

'Look!' shouted Tim.

He disappeared over the top of the muddy bank. It dropped down very steeply at this point. Tim skidded the last bit and landed on a pebbly foreshore. Then Ben

landed with a scrunch beside him. Just behind was Jax, slithering down the mud-slide with his forelegs comically splayed out.

Ben followed Tim's gaze and whistled excitedly.

'Wonder if we can get through?' he said.

Mini arrived next, then Ludo and Amy. Amy slipped and fell, coming down the steep bank. Ben quickly gave her a hand up.

'What's Tim found?' asked Amy, struggling to her feet.

'It's a tunnel!' explained Ben. 'The stream goes into a tunnel.'

Some way ahead of them, the stream gushed and gurgled into a tiny tunnel. It was no more than a very large pipe really, perhaps a metre-and-a-half in diameter. The pipe ran above ground for twenty metres and then disappeared under Bridge Street.

'So that's how the stream gets into her grounds!' said Mini, looking excited. Ben was already getting his Stingray torch out of the back pocket of his jeans.

'I'm going in,' he said.

'I'll go first!' said Mini, snatching the torch from him. 'You might get stuck, Ben. I'll go and see if it's OK!'

Before anyone could stop her, she went splashing down the stream, ducked her head and dived into the tunnel, the torch beam shining brightly.

Good old Mini. The all waded into the water and crowded round the entrance. Bending down, they could peer inside and watch the progress of Mini's silhouette, a black shape moving in the torch's glow, and hear the slip-slop of boots through water, echoing eerily. It must be very slippery in there.

Then the crouching silhouette and the torchlight disappeared round the curve of the pipe and all was black for a while.

'Hope she's OK,' said Ludo.

'Oh, come *on*, Min,' muttered Amy tensely, as the seconds ticked by. Why did each second seem like a minute?

'I'll go in and find her –' began Tim.

'No,' said Ben. 'I'll go, with Jax –'

And then, suddenly, they all cheered as a glow of light reappeared from round the far bend. It was travelling this way. They heard the welcome slip-slop of Mini's boots as she worked her way back up the tunnel. Behind the bobbing light there was only blackness, but the light was coming nearer and nearer.

Finally Mini emerged amongst them. She arched her back, laughing, looking elated.

'It's OK! We can all get through! It's not as small as it looks. Water's a bit deep in places. Come on, what are we waiting for? We can walk straight under Bridge Street and into her grounds!'

Bent almost double, Hands plunged into the tunnel. Ben was leading the way, with Jax on the leash; the torch in his other hand. The dog kept letting out excited little growls and splashing the walls as he ran. It was like an echo chamber in there. Their whispers and laughter ran ahead of them, then came bouncing back.

At one point, where the pipe curved round the bend, somewhere under Bridge Street, Amy slipped into deeper water and got two bootfuls. But she struggled out of the other end of the tunnel with the rest of them. They were relieved to see daylight. And their backs were really aching!

'See!' whispered Mini in glee. 'We're right inside her grounds now!'

They blinked and looked around cautiously. Ben extinguished his torch and replaced it in his back pocket.

They were standing on a pebbly foreshore, not unlike the one they'd left behind. But here the banks of the stream sloped gently and were neat and cultivated. There were some bay trees, some ornamental rose-bushes and, along the top of the bank, at eye-level, a line of flowering shrubs.

Cautiously, they scrambled up the bank, then crouched behind the shrubs. They parted them and peered through.

Ahead of them the back lawns of Greenacre sloped gently up to the house. There was Cleopatra's run, by the back drive, just in front of the kitchens.

Jax let out a low growl. Ben instantly clamped his muzzle with both hands. Jax knew what that meant. *No barking. Not a sound.*

'Good boy!' whispered Ben, and slipped a piece of fudge in the dog's mouth. Then he handed the bag round. Fudge had never tasted so good.

'Well, looks all clear,' said Tim excitedly, keeping his voice low.

They were relieved to see that, upstairs at the back of the house, the blinds were drawn. And downstairs was an unmistakable air of stillness. Mrs Hopp-Daniels was not yet up.

'OK,' nodded Ludo. 'Just you two go. It shouldn't take long for Jax to get the scent.'

'We'll put him in the run and get him to niff the hutch,' said Ben. 'That's where the strongest scent'll be. Come on, Tim.'

As those two tiptoed off up the wet lawn with Jax, the other three waited behind the flowering shrubs. Amy managed to get her boots off, one by one, and tip all the water out. She watched it trickle down the slope below.

Then, with Mini and Ludo, she settled down on her haunches to watch and see what Jax would do.

chapter 8

Amy Breaks Ranks

*B*en bent down. He opened the little gate
into Cleopatra's empty enclosure. Then he
let go of Jax's leash and pushed the dog
inside.

'In you go!' he whispered. 'Go and get a
good niff!'

Jax bounded up and down happily,
inside the run, then came back to the gate.
He peered up at Ben and wagged his tail.

'Go and niff the hutch, you silly nut!'
hissed Ben.

The hutch was at the far end of the run.
Tim tiptoed round the outside of the wire
netting, until he drew level with it. He
pushed his hand through a hole in the
netting, in order to give the rabbit's wooden
sleeping quarters a sharp tap.

'Come on, boy!' Tim called softly. 'Down this end!'

Tongue hanging out, Jax lolloped down to the empty hutch to see what Tim was on about. He sniffed all round it, then put his head in the open front. He buried his nose in Cleopatra's bed of straw. Now his tail started to wag excitedly and he gave a long, low whine. He'd picked up the scent, at last. Rabbit!

'OK. Here, Jax!' hissed Ben. He glanced nervously towards the house but the blinds were still drawn. All was silent as the grave. 'Come on, boy. You've got it!'

Jax nosed the ground inside the run and would have liked to stay a bit longer. But as soon as he passed near the gate, Ben grabbed his trailing leash and yanked him outside.

'OK. Find. Find!' he commanded.

'Wonder which way she went?' whispered Tim in excitement. Both boys watched the dog eagerly as he nosed around outside the run busily. He was trying hard to pick up the trail.

'*Find!*' repeated Ben.

But Jax was looking bewildered. Eager to please Ben, he ran hither and thither, hunting in the moisture-laden grass. The

88

boys took him on the lead all the way
round the run and he continued urgently
to seek. His black nose was wet and shiny
by now, yet he couldn't seem to pick up
the trail.

One spot looked promising, where there
was a hole in the wire netting and some
matted angora clinging to it nearby. Was
this the point of escape? But still Jax drew
a blank. No trail. He let out one or two
growls of frustration, then finally gave up.

He shook himself, sat down on the wet
grass and yawned.

Ben and Tim looked at each other in
dismay, just as Ludo emerged from the

shrubs, shaking his head and frowning.

'We've all been stupid,' said Ludo. 'We forgot about the rain!'

Empress Cleopatra had escaped before that downpour last night, hadn't she? No wonder poor old Jax couldn't pick up the scent.

The rain must have washed it clean away.

For the next hour, they combed the grounds of Greenacre House. It was nerve-racking, especially having to creep round the front. There was very little cover here and early-morning traffic passed the gates. The had to fling themselves flat when the milkman's float came up the drive, and again when the post van arrived. It was a relief to get round to the back again.

They hunted round trees, through flower-beds, under bushes. All the time they hoped that in sheltered places, where the ground was less wet, Jax might happen upon Cleopatra's trail for them. But he didn't.

'Mrs Hoppitt *definitely* told us that Cleo never goes far,' Mini whispered in frustration. 'Didn't she, Amy?'

'Yes, that's what she *said*,' replied Amy. She wriggled her toes furiously inside her wet boots. She was trying to get her feet warm.

'So she's got to be here *somewhere*,' gritted Tim.

'Well, she isn't,' stated Ludo.

Of a fluffed-up, fun-loving bundle of golden angora there was no sign. Although unable to pick up the trail, Jax would certainly have noticed any movements. He'd yanked the lead out of Ben's hand to go chasing after a scampering hedgehog! It had eluded him by rolling itself up into a prickly ball beneath a beech hedge.

'Lu's right,' said Ben. 'Looks like Cleo got a travel bug.'

'Walkin' where rabbit has never walked before!' joked Amy.

'Or just decided to go into town and meet her public!' commented Ludo.

They all grinned. But Tim, being Tim-like, was quick to get down to business again.

'OK. So we've got to find out which way she went. She wouldn't like it out the front, because of the traffic.'
Greenacre's gates were near a crossroads.
'She'd head for open fields. Is there any place she could get out easily?'

They'd come over the wrought-iron bridge to the far side of the stream some minutes earlier, leaving the bottom part of the grounds till last. Now they were lolling against the high wall at the very bottom. It was the same wall that turned at right angles and ran up along Bridge Street. From here, they scanned the scene.

Well, Cleopatra wouldn't have escaped under Bridge Street, the way they'd come in. That was certain. And after crossing the grounds, the stream disappeared under a fence. This close-boarded fence ran the length of Greenacre and separated it from the next house along, in River Lane. It looked very solid; Cleo couldn't get through there.

'I think it's the water-meadows behind here,' said Tim, turning and touching the wall behind them. 'She'd like those! This wall looks old. Maybe it's got some holes in it.'

Hands started exploring along the wall. It was twice their own height, covered in Virginia creeper. There were chunks of broken glass along the top, at intervals, to deter intruders. Well, she couldn't have gone over the top anyway! Any gaps along the bottom?

Bending down, they started to feel their way along the foot of the wall, pulling trailing creeper and tussocks of grass aside, looking for holes in the brickwork. It was Amy who happened to glance up and look back towards the house. The blinds were no longer closed!

'Better be careful,' she whispered. 'I think she must have got up –'

'Look at these drainage pipes!' Ben was exclaiming in excitement. He'd discovered some wide, hollow pipes going through the wall at ground level. There was a long line of them. 'She could've squeezed through one of these, easy! Bet this is how she got out –'

'Shut up, Ben!' warned Ludo.

'Question is,' whispered Mini, 'how do *we* get out?'

Because suddenly they could hear voices. Some boys had appeared at the back of the house. They were standing by the kitchen door and talking to Mrs Hopp-Daniels. And Mrs Hopp-Daniels's voice carried clearly.

'I'd like you to search the water-meadows, please. I certainly don't want you trampling round my gardens! I've searched those myself and I shall be searching them again –'

Bounty-hunters!'

Eager to pinch *their* £100!

The ugly face of competition!

They heard the back door slam and then the boys' voices fade away up the front drive.

But Tim's main interest was in the rabbit-sized bolt-holes that Ben had just discovered.

'Yes, she's in the water-meadows. Bet you!' he mouthed.

'We've got to get out of here, fast!' Mini repeated. 'Mrs Hoppitt's up!'

Ben eyed the high wall. Just to his left was a good, strong main stem of creeper, and a useful buttress. And, above those, a considerable gap in the line of broken glass!

'Quick, you lot! Over the top!' he whispered. 'I'll manage Jax. I'll come last!'

One by one, they shot up to the top of the wall. There was a sheer drop the other side, especially daunting for Mini. But they launched themselves down and parachute-landed, the way they'd been taught in PE.

Jax was a problem. He stood shivering on top of the wall and whining. But Ben scooped him up in his arms, like a baby, and they jumped together. Whoomph! They crashed down into the long grass and rolled over together, Ben laughing, Jax licking his face in gratitude.

They were in the water-meadows.

So, it seemed, were quite a lot of other people.

They could see them dotted around in the distance, mainly in little groups: some in small swarms, others strung out. They were heading in different directions – the River Arms, Old Inn Lane, the river tow-path, the distant woods. Some had dogs with them. Some carried cardboard boxes to put the rabbit in. One man held aloft a large shrimp-net, perhaps the better to catch it with.

'Oh no!' said Mini, gazing at the scene in horror.

'The ravening hordes have descended,' said Ludo wryly.

'Maybe we'd have thought of coming here sooner, if we'd had our map!' said Tim crossly. 'Still, nobody's found her yet, have they? That's obvious!'

'We're not going to let a bit of competition put us off,' declared Ben.

Only Amy was silent.

'You bet we're not!' stated Tim. He was on his mettle. There was a very determined glint in his eye. 'Come on. Quick march! Let's spread out in a line. We'll work every bit of ground. We won't let any of *them* beat us! Not after all this!'

They strung out in a line and started to march forward. Then, suddenly, Amy stopped dead.

She was breaking ranks.

'I'm going home!' she exclaimed. She was looking at her watch. 'Else I'll be late for Gym Club!'

Tim walked back and gazed at his twin sister in amazement.

'Gym Club?' he said furiously. 'What, when we're in the middle of a case?'

They all gathered round.

'We can't give up *now*, Amy!' protested Mini. 'You know that reward's our only hope.'

'Activities aren't that important, Amy. Let's have a vote –' began Ludo tactfully.

'They *are* important and it's *not* our only hope. I'm not asking anyone else to come, but I've got faith in Mr Amazing even if nobody else has! And hardly anyone at JVJ even *knows* about him yet! I'm going to spread it all round Clubs this morning – how good he is. Try and get round people! Get them to come and see him! So there's no point in having a vote because I'm going anyway!'

Amy turned on her heel.

The other four looked at each other. So

that was it! It wasn't anything to do with missing Gym Club. It was all to do with Mr Amazing. But she just wasn't being practical! Most people at JVJ were as broke as *they* were and, besides, by now they'd have other things arranged! So what was the point?

Tim grabbed her muddy sleeve and tried to pull her back.

'Let her go if she wants to, Tim!' snapped Ben. He liked Amy a lot. Even when he thought she was being silly.

'Bye!' shouted Amy.

She ran directly ahead across the water-meadows, towards Old Inn Lane. Didn't that lead back into Bridge Street? It'd be quite a run, going home via the roads. But she had to get washed and changed before she went to Gym Club. She'd bike to JVJ from home. She'd make it in time. She was a fast runner.

Regretfully, the other Hands watched the running figure bobbing off into the distance. There was a lot of ground to cover and now they were one short.

'He said he was going to *magic* the crowds along! She seems to have forgotten that!' Tim snorted.

'Well, maybe she wants to give the magic a helping hand,' sighed Mini.

Jax barked and jerked on the lead, eager to get on.

So, leaving Amy to run home, they fanned out across the long, lush grass. Their eyes and ears were attuned, ready for the smallest movement.

Somewhere, they hoped not too far away, was the elusive Empress Cleopatra. A valuable, golden-haired rabbit: fluffy, glossy and full of herself. How they longed to see those twitching ears and that goofy face! Not the athletic sort – was she? – but tame and spoiled and used to a life of luxury. Not the sort to venture too far into the wilds, you'd think!

So where was she?

Ben, Tim, Mini and Ludo were determined to find her. Before the competition did. Even if it took all morning.

Tim squared his jaw.

'You can run but you can't hide, rabbit,' he said, to rally the troops.

chapter 9

Tension Mounts

'**T**he banner's changed!' exclaimed Amy, as she walked into the school hall at the end of the morning. She'd been intending to have a last peep in there; make sure everything was still shipshape for their Grand Jumble Sale.

'Like it, Amy?' asked Mr Gage. 'Haven't they done a good job?'

'It's brilliant, sir!' gasped Amy, with pleasure.

She'd had a reasonable morning at JVJ. She'd told everyone at Gym Club about Mr Amazing. Some of them were doing other things. But one or two had promised to come along, if the rain held off and they could get hold of some money to spend.

At break, Amy had tracked down members of Chess Club and Computer Club, lolling round by the drinks machine.

Chris Bundy and some others had said that magic was corny. But again, a few promised that they'd try to come.

She went to look for Art Club but they weren't in their usual place, the school art and crafts room.

It was only now, when she looked into the hall, that she realized. Art Club had been working in there all morning, at Mr Gage's instigation.

They'd been working on 6A's banner, which still hung, mural-like, across the back of the school stage.

There were two members of Art Club left. They stood in the body of the hall, admiring the banner. With them were Mr Gage and the headmaster, Mr Morton, who'd just dropped in.

The banner looked wonderful. It was clever what they'd done. They'd overpainted the words *As featured in the local press* with dazzling coloured stars, crescent moons and lightning flashes, thus obliterating those pathetic words.

In the white space below, in huge letters, they'd painted on a new message:

MR AMAZING – THE WORLD'S GREATEST MAGICIAN

The headmaster turned to greet Amy.
His car was parked outside the hall. He
was on his way to a conference for the rest
of the day. But he'd very much wanted to
look in and see how Class 6A's effort was
coming along.

'Excellent, isn't it?' he said. 'It's going
out by the school gates. I've given special
permission. Anyone passing with small
children won't be able to resist it.'

Then he placed a hand on Amy's
shoulder and smiled.

'I've been hearing all about your misfortunes, from Mr Gage. You and your friends have done magnificently to conjure up a magician from nowhere. Well done, Amy!'

'Let's hope the rain keeps off, sir,' replied Amy shyly, feeling a little glow of pleasure at his words.

'Yes. Fingers crossed. Well, I must dash now. Good luck for this afternoon.'

As soon as he'd gone, Amy turned and thanked Mr Gage.

'I think it's really good!' she exclaimed. 'And it'll be really great, having it outside!'

'Paint's still wet, but it'll have to do,' replied her teacher. 'Had to do *something*, didn't we, Amy? I take it you tuned into *Round-Up* last night?'

'Yes.' Amy nodded. 'What a let-down. Tim nearly went bananas when he heard it, sir.'

'That rabbit again!' said Gagey. He looked angry. 'Unbelievable!'

'But Mr Amazing's staying at our house,' Amy told him proudly. 'Mum's been feeding him up for this afternoon.'

'Really?' Mr Gage laughed. 'Good. Good.'

Amy stayed on to help fix the banner

up outside, just by the school gates. She got some paint on her hands, but it couldn't be helped. Then they wound some bunting in and out of the iron palings. They all admired the result. Mort was right. The banner was excellent. And it *would* make passers-by want to come inside, especially Mums with children.

It was magical!

Amy fetched her bike to go home. Mr Gage's car was parked near the Back Lane gate. It was nearly one o'clock.

'Right, a quick dash home for some lunch now,' he said, as he opened his car door. 'Remember, everybody back here by a quarter to two. We've got to be ready to open at two o'clock sharp. Didn't the others want to come to activities this morning?'

When Amy explained about the rabbit, Gagey's face hardened.

'I wouldn't go and find that woman's rabbit for her, not even for £1000! On principle, I wouldn't,' he said. He'd played snooker with his friend, the editor, last night, who'd been very, very angry about Mrs Hopp-Daniels messing about with his lovely front page. He'd said it wasn't the first time, and sometimes he wished he could find another paper to edit. 'However,'

Mr Gage relented, 'I suppose it's very enterprising of them. I can see it's worth a try.'

'Oh, I shouldn't think they've found it, sir,' said Amy cheerfully. She turned her handlebars and wheeled her red cycle through the gate, ready to dash for home. 'The whole town's out looking!'

As she pedalled fast towards the Knoll House, she passed some of them – three boys from 4A. They were carrying some green netting, like Mum put over the soft fruit bushes in summer. They were exhausted-looking and had long faces.

But nobody's face was longer than Tim's.

He said goodbye to the others and let himself into the kitchen only ten minutes ahead of Amy. He was cold, muddy, bedraggled and fed up. Just like Mini. And just like Ben and Ludo, who were also starving hungry. Those two had missed breakfast – and the bag of fudge was long gone.

In Back Lane, they'd met Kate Roberts, cycling back from a trip to Tesco for her mum. She'd looked at them, screwed up her freckled nose and giggled:

'Been looking for that rabbit? Can't your Mr Amazing find it for us? Or isn't he as amazing as all that!'

Tim could have killed her.

He crept into the kitchen and saw that Dad was in there alone, with his back turned. He was looking after a big cauldron of soup on the Aga. Having a taste of it, mainly. Mum was upstairs, getting Harry up from his cot after a sleep.

A magician living in the garden was too much for little bruv. Just thinking about Mr Amazing had made him over-excited. He'd collapsed, exhausted and screeching, by mid-morning, because he couldn't get sugar lumps to appear in teddy's paws, the way Mr Amazing could. Mum felt that having recklessly promised to take him to the 'bajic' show this afternoon, he'd first better have a long nap.

Tim slipped his muddy boots off, then tried to sneak past Dad, into the hall. But Dad looked round.

'Tim! What a sight you look. Go and have a hot bath and get into some clean clothes. It's almost lunch-time. And then you've got to go out!'

'That's just where I'm going, Dad. I feel like a hot bath. I'm freezing,' replied Tim.

He took his muddy anorak off, then climbed up to his bedroom on the attic floor and found some clean clothes. He then came down to the first floor. From the airing cupboard, which was heated by the Aga, he pulled out the thickest, warmest bath towel he could find.

But when he reached the bathroom, he heard someone singing loudly in the bath and happy splashing sounds. It was Mr Amazing! Tim scowled. He'd already been locked out of his own HQ. Now he found himself locked out of his own bathroom, too!

'I expect he's just having a lovely long soak,' said Mum indulgently, when Tim peered into Harry's bedroom to complain about it. Mum was hunting in a drawer for a clean track suit for Harry. 'I gave him lunch early. He loved my soup, Tim! Then he asked if he could have a bath. He had his costume with him, in a suitcase. Still in there, then?'

'Bajic man in suitcase?' asked Harry sleepily.

'No, Harry!' laughed Tim.

'Tim. You're a mess!' exclaimed Mrs Dalladay, glancing up at him. 'You'd better go and see if you can get the downstairs shower to work.'

*

Long after he'd finished his bath, Mr
Amazing remained in the bathroom. For
him, an appearance was a rare occurrence
these days. He was taking infinite pains to
look his best. So he didn't appear until the
very last: just as the Dalladays were
finishing lunch; only minutes before the
twins had to leave for JVJ.

It was going to be a dramatic entry. He
looked so good it was going to amaze them.

By the time he appeared, Tim's spirits
were already much revived. True, the
shower had been tepid and kept going off,
while Mr Amazing ran off more hot water
upstairs. But it was good to be in clean
clothes and feel warm again. The
minestrone soup and crusty French bread
were delicious; so was the large cream
doughnut he finished up with, washed
down with a mug of hot tea.

Mum and Dad listened with great
sympathy as he recounted the heartaches
and woe of the morning's quest, as though
he were a knight who'd been through fire
and water in search of the Holy Grail, only
to return empty-handed (which was true,
in a way). Of course, he didn't mention the
bit about trespassing in the grounds of
Greenacre House first.

When Amy left them, they'd gone on to search a wide area. After hunting through the water-meadows they'd walked along the tow-path by the River Jug for miles, explored fields and woods, hope fading all the while; and finally returned via the bridle-way and Letcombe Lane.

'Wonder if it could have fallen in the river?' said Mum. 'It won't be used to the wild.'

'Doubt it,' said Dad. 'It can't be that stupid. So, no reward, eh, Tim?'

'Nope.'

Then Amy told them all her news: the banner being changed and putting it up outside and how Mr Morton had congratulated them. She also reported on her own quest – how she'd told as many people as possible about Mr Amazing and begged them to come.

'Just as well you did, Amy,' Tim now admitted grudgingly.

They were all sitting round the big pine table, unaware that behind them the door from the hall was opening.

Suddenly Harry, whose high chair faced that way, went pink with excitement, banged his spoon on his tray and screeched, *'Bajic man!'*

They all glanced round. Amy gasped. There stood Mr Amazing, no longer in frayed suit and worn-out shoes, which were now in a small suitcase beside him, but utterly transformed.

From his polished knee-high red boots with pointed toes to the red silk top hat rammed over his shock of grey curls, he looked more magician-like than ever before. A king above all other magicians. The whole Dalladay family stared transfixed at his swirling, star-spangled cloak: rich, silken, voluminous, studded with little semiprecious stones. It was an old, old cloak, but very beautiful and mysterious. From out of its folds he stretched his hands: long, tapering, magician's hands. In one of them was a small wand.

'Greetings!' he cried.

The Dalladays all clapped his entrance and he bowed.

Dad was impressed. 'How did you pack that tall top hat in a suitcase?' he asked.

Politely, Mr Amazing removed the top hat. He slapped the crown with the magic wand and − *flip!* − it concertinaed down to nothing and disappeared up his sleeve.

'Hat donn!' laughed Harry. 'Do it again!'

But Mr Amazing was anxious to return to the caravan.

'I go to contemplate now, in deep peace. I shall make my final mental preparation. I shall arrive at your school later, when all the crowds have gathered.' He smiled at Tim. 'When everything is in full swing and the excitement is at its height. At what time shall I make my grand entrance?'

'Say half-past two?' suggested Tim hopefully. 'That gives people time to spend some money first.'

'Yes, that's a good time,' nodded Amy.

It was agreed that Mr Amazing would pack up the caravan and drive along to JVJ in his van. He'd park it at the back of the hall. Perhaps the committee would be kind enough to let him in through the little door and take him to the ante-room, just off stage? There he'd get everything ready before stepping out magnificently on stage.

'And this afternoon, I shall perform magic undreamt of,' he stated. His popping blue eyes were shining brightly as he stared at Amy. 'All your problems will be solved. The men will get their new lifeboat! After that –'

He smiled a mysterious, secretive smile.

'– after that, I shall be gone. You shall never see me, nor the likes of me, again!'

He walked over to Mrs Dalladay, bowed low and kissed her hand.

'Thank you for your hospitality, madam. It has been memorable.'

'Our pleasure!'

Humming happily to himself, Mr Amazing then let himself out of the back door. They heard him go to the van and lock his suitcase inside. Then they heard the tap-tap-tap of his pointed boots as his footsteps receded down the garden path towards the caravan, his inner sanctum.

Harry just sat in his high chair, his mouth opening and closing, speechless with pleasure.

Tim was the first to find his voice. He looked relieved.

'Hey, he looks good now, doesn't he? Now he's all dressed up!'

'He certainly does,' agreed Dad.

'I wonder if he *will* solve your problems?' mused Mum.

'Well, he's certainly trying hard, Mum,' said Tim.

'No! More than that. He seems so sure. As though he's actually capable of real magic. I do believe he is!' Mrs Dalladay sipped her tea thoughtfully and wondered if she might have fallen, ever so slightly, under some kind of spell. After all, she hadn't really meant to invite him to supper. And she certainly hadn't *intended* to make the twins lend him their caravan . . .

As he glanced at his mother's face Tim realized that he might have been wrong when he'd said to Amy: *He couldn't even magic himself some food and a bed for the night.* Because he had. From Mum. And a hot bath as well!

Then Amy spoke.

'Of *course* he's capable of real magic, Mum. He's promised.'

Yet there was a tiny knot of tension inside her. A mounting tension that she couldn't explain.

'Well, let's get cleared away, shall we?' said Dad briskly. 'You twins have to go in a minute. Teapots coming to call for you?'

As he and Amy stacked some dishes on the draining-board together, Dad glanced out through the kitchen window. He could see dark storm clouds gathering but didn't want to think about them.

'Well, your magic man's being very kind and generous, isn't he, Amy?' he admitted. 'Let's hope a good crowd turns up for him.'

Amy nodded. 'Yes, Dad.' She suddenly understood the reason for her tension.

Just after that Mini arrived, followed by Ben and Ludo, who'd heard Mr Amazing singing to himself in HQ and given it a wide berth. Ben had left Jax behind, of course, totally exhausted and fast asleep in his dog-basket.

Handles & Spouts set off from the Knoll House at exactly twenty minutes to two. Ludo carried two old jumpers of Anya's for the second-hand clothes stall. Amy had some bags of peppermints, which she and Mum had made for the home-made sweets stall. Kate Roberts was organizing the Smarties-in-a-jar.

Mrs Dalladay was going to push Harry along to JVJ in the push-chair, for two o'clock sharp, when the doors opened.

At a quarter to two the nine members of 6A's fund-raising committee waited at the side door of the school hall. Mr Gage had gone to find Mr Reed, the caretaker, to ask him to open up. They all agreed that the banner at the school gates could make all the difference.

Mr Gage returned. Mr Reed fumbled with a big bunch of keys.

Amy felt a very large drop of rain fall on her head, then another.

She looked up in alarm. So did the

others. Then came a brilliant flash of lightning and a deafening crash of thunder, right above their heads.

They got into the hall with only moments to spare before the heavens opened and the rain came sheeting down.

chapter 10

Mr Amazing!

*I*t seemed like the final disaster. Once safely inside the hall, the Jumble Sale committee pressed their noses against the windows and watched in disbelief as the rain poured down. It was falling so heavily they couldn't even see across the playground!

'Just as people would've been setting out to come!' said Tim in total despair. 'They won't bother now.'

'You're right, Tim. Nobody comes to jumble sales late!' wailed Emily. 'They'll just think they've missed all the bargains and'll stay at home and watch telly!'

'Rain looks set in, anyway,' groaned Ben, as another clap of thunder sounded above.

'It's going to be a flop,' pronounced Marcus moodily. 'Flop of the year!' He turned on Ben and hissed, 'Stupid idea in the first place. Everyone's fed up with the

Lifeboat Appeal. Now we're all going to
look stupid.'

'You're stupid already!' raged Ben,
grabbing hold of Marcus's tie.

'That'll do, Ben!' said Mr Gage, not
knowing how much he'd been provoked.

'Mum won't be able to walk Harry in
this,' Amy whispered to Mini, 'and our car's
gone to the garage for a service!' Her lower
lip was trembling. She was thinking that if
Harry, Mr Amazing's greatest fan, wasn't
going to make it, who was?

At this rate, he'd be coming on stage to

face an empty hall. She felt like sitting down and crying.

'Come on, Ame,' said Mini kindly. She yanked hold of her hand and dragged her away from the window. 'Let's go and have a peep up the corridor! Let's see if anyone got here early!'

After letting them into the hall, Mr Reed had hurried off to open up the school's main doors. If there were any early arrivals, he couldn't let them queue outside in the rain, he'd said. He'd let them in and they could wait in the entrance hall.

'Look!' said Mini, as they walked up the corridor.

At the far end, beyond the glass swing-doors, they could glimpse some figures huddled in the entrance hall! They quickened their pace and went to peer through the glass. It couldn't quite be called a queue; just a small gaggle.

There were four elderly ladies, with plastic carrier-bags, who lived near Packers Bridge. They'd seen the notice in Dolly's and never missed a jumble. And three boys from Gym Club, persuaded to come by Amy. Good! All had left home early, just before the storm, to be first in the queue. All had got soaked through, half-way along Bridge Street.

118

Beyond, through the glass panels of the main doors, were wobbling images through water-dashed glass of cars parked in the playground, figures huddled inside them. A few top juniors, with parents, waiting to dash in at two o'clock.

'See! Not too bad!' said Mini. 'It's a start.'

Amy nodded. Then she caught sight of the banner. It had fallen down by the gates in a soggy heap, all its bright colours melding together and running off in little rivulets into the puddle where it lay.

'The banner!' moaned Amy. 'We should have tried to save it!'

At five minutes to two, with the rain still lashing down, Mr Gage shrugged and told Dom to go and let people in.

'If they're not here by now, they aren't coming anyway,' he said.

Mr Gage and Mini manned the door, collecting 10p pieces in admission money. Amy and Ludo stood to attention behind the second-hand bookstall and watched the public enter.

It was still the same people as before.

'Not the eighty people we reckoned we needed,' said Ludo.

'Not even eighteen,' replied Amy.

And at the bric-à-brac stall next door, Marcus scowled and muttered to himself, 'Well, I like that. Mum hasn't bothered to come herself.'

The thunder receded, but the heavy rain continued. After twenty minutes, Ludo and Amy had only had three customers for second-hand books. The elderly ladies preferred coats and jumpers and the Gym Club boys preferred home-made sweets. Ludo was haggling with David Marshall over the Asterix. It cost 20p and Dave had only 10p, but Ludo let him have it in the end.

Amy was busy counting heads. Four more people had braved the weather and driven to JVJ, including Mrs Minter, Mini's divorced mum. And Mr Reed had kindly gone and collected his wife and mother-in-law from the caretaker's bungalow nearby, even though it meant getting wet. Of Mrs Dalladay and Harry there was still no sign, of course. As for passers-by . . . hardly!

'I make it nineteen,' she told Ludo. 'We've got nineteen people and there's ten of us, counting Mr Gage. So that's twenty-nine altogether!'

She was hoping, anxiously, that an audience of twenty-nine would be magical enough for Mr Amazing to make things happen, as he'd promised. She decided that she must continue to have faith in him. She looked at her watch and checked it with the big clock. It was exactly twenty past two. At this moment, she realized, Mr Amazing would be leaving HQ behind for ever, walking up to the house to climb into his van . . . That led to a new worry.

'Oh, Lu, he's wearing his precious magician's clothes!' exclaimed Amy. 'You know, the ones we told you about! They're going to get soaked through!'

'I don't think so, somehow!' said Ludo suddenly. He nodded his head towards the doors, his reddish fringe flopping. 'Something tells me the rain must've stopped!'

'Oh, everyone's leaving!' gasped Amy, becoming aware of a mad scramble towards the door. She turned and looked through the window. Ludo was right. The sky was dark but the rain had stopped, as suddenly and dramatically as it had started. 'Why? Just because it's stopped raining!'

Even the three boys from Gym Club were sneaking out. They'd like to have seen the magician but nothing was any fun in wet clothes. Only Mrs Minter and the Marshall family remained.

'Well, to get home before the next cloudburst, I suppose,' said Ludo. 'Should be OK for a while now. At least Mr Amazing'll be able to get here now. Without ruining his clothes.'

True enough, when the twins met Mr Amazing at the stage door ten minutes later, he was perfectly dry from top hat down to pointed toes. So were Mrs Dalladay and Harry, who climbed out from the other side of the van.

Mum led Harry off to the main entrance. Squealing happily and wanting to jump in the playground puddles in his wellington boots, the little boy was in a state of high excitement. Mr Magic had made the rain stop, Mum had explained, drying his tears for him, and was going to magic them to school in his van. And now here they were!

'Greetings,' said Mr Amazing, as soon as he saw Tim and Amy. He walked towards them, carrying a box of secrets under his arm and waving his wand; a truly fantastic-looking figure.

They took him in the back way and left him by the door of the ante-room, next to

the stage. He told them he'd make his
grand entry on to the stage very shortly.

'I need a few moments, just to collect my
mental powers together,' he said, opening
the door of the ante-room. 'And everything
is in full swing, yes? A good crowd awaits
me?'

'It – it's a bit sparse, sir,' said Tim,
looking acutely embarrassed.

'We're ever so sorry, sir,' said Amy. She
gazed at that wonderful cloak, so old and
precious. He truly must have magic powers.
Those eyes of his! But who was there to see
them? She was suddenly overcome with
shame. 'We've let you down. Our – our
publicity just wasn't good enough. And we
couldn't even make the weather come right!'

A tear rolled down her cheek. But Mr
Amazing seemed quite calm. He lifted his
wand and touched Amy lightly on the
cheek with it.

'I am the magician, not you. If the world
has never recognized my greatness, then so
be it. That is the way of the world.' Those
popping blue eyes met hers, no longer intense,
but gentle. 'You worry too much, my child.'

Humming softly to himself, he entered
the ante-room and closed the door.

*

The sparse little audience found his stage presence quite awe-inspiring. Each amazing illusion was greeted with cheers and heartfelt applause. Harry was transfixed by it all.

So were they all, but even so, between illusions, Tim and several others couldn't stop doing frantic sums in their heads. What had they made today? £20 perhaps? £25? Certainly not the £100 they'd talked about, that the whole school would be expecting to hear about on Monday. What failures they were going to look!

Amy didn't bother to do sums in her head. She just kept tingling with expectation and wondering by what magical means Mr Amazing was going to rescue the situation.

For his very last feat, he asked Mr Gage to come up on stage and blindfold him. He disappeared off to the ante-room and collected the blindfold, while the teacher was mounting the steps.

As Gagey tied the blindfold round Mr Amazing's eyes, the magician held his arms aloft, his palms resting on top of his magnificent red top hat, as though to make sure it was rammed tightly over his shock of grey curls.

'The feat I am about to perform,' announced the blindfolded magician, as the teacher stepped down off the stage, 'will truly astound you. It demands such intense mental powers that only rarely can I perform it. And only then if the planets are in a favourable aspect and the energy fields are strong. Today is such a day. My grandfather once performed this feat for the Tsar of all the Russias and today I shall perform it for you!'

The audience became very still, very tense. All of them, not just Amy alone, had the feeling that something very, very special was about to happen. The magician seemed to be under intense mental strain. Even his breathing was becoming laboured.

'What is this feat, you ask? I shall tell you. It is in my powers to grant one of you a wish. However impossible the wish, I shall grant it, here in front of your very eyes. You may wish for anything! But only one person will be chosen. One person alone, and their wish shall be granted!'

Amy drew in a deep breath. A strange little tingle was running up and down her spine.

'But who shall that person be, you ask? I will tell you. The one who wishes the truest

and wishes the hardest and truly believes in
the power of magic! My wand will quiver
and quiver as it seeks that person out. Now,
total silence, all of you. Watch my wand
carefully. And please begin to wish –
NOW!'

As Mr Amazing stood blindfolded on the
stage, he passed his wand backwards and
forwards along the faces of the audience
below. It was quivering and twitching in
his long magician's fingers. The strain that
the feat was putting on his powers could be
clearly seen. Perspiration was breaking out
all over his face. His very hat seemed to
sway and move from the energy waves sent
out by his brain. Amy watched that wand
moving and twitching and suddenly felt a
deep sense of joy.

Everything was going to be all right. She
just *knew* it was. She'd always thought it
would be. Somehow, Mr Amazing was
going to make everything come right for
them.

She stood gazing at the trembling wand
and wished and wished and *wished*. As she
did so, the wand became very still and –

There could be no mistake about it.

It was pointed directly at Amy.

Amy exhaled her breath in relief. And

now, Mr Amazing was pulling his blindfold
down, to see to whom his wand pointed.
Then he asked Amy to step forward to the
foot of the stage.

'So you are to be the chosen one!' he
said. 'You, my dear, shall have your wish
granted. What is it, that wish? Speak it out
loud to us, loud and clear, so that all may
hear it.'

'*To make £100, sir!*' Amy cried, simply
bursting to get it out. 'So the men will have
their new lifeboat, like you said they
would!'

'Then your wish is granted.'

He removed his top hat and walked to the front of the stage. A pair of golden-tufted ear tips suddenly poked up from inside the hat. There were shouts of amazement and astonishment from the audience.

'Wabbit!' cried Harry, chuckling and clapping his hands. 'Do it some more!'

Mr Amazing gently lifted the doe out of the hat by her ears. He bent down and placed her in Amy's arms.

It was Empress Cleopatra.

'Cleo!' whispered Amy, feeling quite stunned. The doe looked up at her with soft eyes and nuzzled in the crook of her arm. Amy stroked the rabbit's beautiful superfine coat, as clean and bright and lustrous as ever. 'Oh, aren't you lovely.'

With shouts and screams of excitement, everybody was gathering round Amy and the rabbit. Nobody noticed Mr Amazing tiptoe quietly off across the stage.

'You can go and collect the reward now, Amy!' cried Tim. 'That's how he's made your wish come true. Oh, isn't this brill!'

'Remarkable,' said Mr Gage, smiling broadly.

'It's really *her*!' whispered Mini, looking

as stunned as Amy and running a hand down Cleo's back.

'She's not really fat,' said Amy. 'It's just the way her coat's all fluffy and sticking out.'

Ben and Ludo were just speechless.

'You lot are brilliant,' said Emily, elbowing her way through.

'Yes, aren't we!' said Tim happily. 'Brilliant to have found Mr Amazing!'

'How *did* you fix it?' asked Marcus, humbled by the sheer unexpectedness of it all.

'Yes, how?' exclaimed Kate. '*I* know! You *did* find her this morning! You just pretended you didn't!'

'Really clever! Giving it to Mr Amazing for his show!' said Dom. 'What a great idea. Wish the whole school could've been here. Wouldn't that have been great —'

'What *are* you all talking about?' asked Amy crossly. 'Don't you believe in magic, any of you? Not even when you see it happen in front of your own eyes?' She looked up at the stage. 'Oh. Where's Mr Amazing gone? We haven't even thanked him yet —'

The she heard a rumbling sound —

A flash of white bodywork and faded

gold lettering went past the windows. The van!

'Mr Amazing!' cried Amy.

She placed Cleopatra into Mini's arms, pushed past everyone and raced out of the hall. As she reached the school gates, the van was just turning right into Bridge Street, away from town, towards open country. The figure at the steering-wheel, back in shimmering cloak, turned his head towards her. He gave Amy a salute and was gone.

Like a figure disappearing back into a dream.

chapter 11

Hip, Hooray for JVJ

Mr Amazing had promised he'd magic the crowds along, which was the bit that Amy had worried about. But that part of his promise came true as well.

As soon as the rain had definitely stopped, people began to emerge in Bridge Street. And some of them saw the Spouts crossing the road from JVJ, with the famous rabbit, accompanied by Mr Gage.

The Handles, standing at the gates, were able to tell passers-by the incredible story (in some triumph, of course). The news spread like wildfire.

The story got a little garbled along the way. Some people rushed along to JVJ expecting to see the rabbit and the magician still there. For this reason the

jumble sale had a stream of visitors in the
last half-hour. Naturally they were
disappointed to find both magician and
rabbit had vanished, but stayed to hunt for
bargains just the same.

Mrs Hopp-Daniels paid up without a
murmur. She wrote out a £100 cheque
for the JVJ Lifeboat Appeal account and
handed it over to Mr Gage. All her
murmurings were reserved for Cleopatra,
whom she held very close to her buxom self,
which was aquiver with joy.

'You've been such a naughty girl, Clee-
Clee. We shall have to do something about
your run. Don't you ever go walkies again!'

Then she hurried off indoors to show her
to the grandchildren.

'Sickening woman,' said Mr Gage as
they walked down the front drive; he
rustled the cheque in his pocket with great
satisfaction.

'I think it's nice she loves her so much!'
protested Amy. She was holding the gilt-
framed photograph of Cleopatra and
planning to put it in her bedroom.

'Yes, she can't be *all* bad, sir,' agreed
Mini.

An expensive-looking Rover car passed
them in the drive. It had a young man at

the wheel and a sticker on the back saying:
THE GREAT MYSTICO IS HERE.

'Well, he might be great but he can't be as great as Mr Amazing,' chortled Mini, glancing back.

'Hear, hear!' said Mr Gage.

In the end, thanks to the late-comers, the Jumble Sale alone raised nearly £80. So on Monday, Mr Morton was able to announce in assembly that they'd not only met their deadline, but dramatically exceeded their target too. That afternoon the school would present the Jugmouth Lifeboat Appeal with a cheque for £1059.50. The *Advertiser* was coming along to take a photograph, to go on this week's front page.

He led the cheers.

'Hip, Hooray for Class 6A! Hip, Hooray for JVJ!' they all shouted, many regretting that they hadn't bothered to come. There'd been a *magician* there and somehow he'd found that famous missing rabbit. He'd actually *produced* it, just like that, out of a hat!

If it weren't for the fact that Arabella Marshall was there and saw the whole thing, you'd swear that the top juniors had made it up! But there again, even Mr Gage said it was true.

And on Friday, the whole story appeared in the *Advertiser*, on the front page. So it *had* to be true!

Mrs Hopp-Daniels was to frown over it, long and hard.

Meanwhile, straight after the jumble sale, Handles & Spouts couldn't wait to get back into HQ. They'd make mugs of tea and eat the jar of Smarties Ludo had won (453 of them) and generally have a celebration.

'You lot go on ahead,' said Amy, when they reached the Knoll House. 'I'll just pop indoors and put Cleo's photo in my bedroom.' She wanted to show it to Mum, too.

Mrs Dalladay and Harry had been home some time. Harry had had a temper-tantrum upon discovering that Mr Amazing had gone out of his life for ever but had now fallen happily asleep in the middle of children's TV.

Ben, Ludo, Tim and Mini entered the caravan and looked round it with satisfaction. Everything exactly as it should be. Not a sign, as Mr Amazing had promised to Amy, that he'd ever existed!

Apart from the open milk carton and the empty sugar puffs packet.

'He must have eaten them all up!' laughed Ludo. 'But at least he's left us some milk for tea! I'll put the kettle on, OK?'

It was great to watch Ludo filling the kettle at the little sink and to know they'd got their HQ back. They were silent for a few moments. Then, for the tenth time that afternoon, Tim said wonderingly, 'How *did* he do it? How *did* he find the rabbit? Mum says he never left the caravan all morning.'

'Maybe it *was* real magic,' said Mini. 'That's what Amy thinks.'

'I know she does,' frowned Tim.

'Well, it is weird, isn't it?' said Ben. 'The way he just came out of nowhere like that and now he's gone back into nowhere. No sign really that anyone's ever been in here. We could have dreamt the whole thing!'

'No sign, except for this,' said Ludo suddenly. He'd noticed something on the floor. Now he bent and picked it up.

He held it out on the palm of his hand for them all to look at. They crowded round and stared in surprise.

It was a fluff of golden angora wool.

Ludo clenched his hand tight round it,

then opened his palm again. The wool
didn't spring back but remained
compressed.

'That's how you tell it's English angora,'
said Ludo, who'd read up on the subject
last night. 'It's because it's superfine.'

They all looked at Ludo in shock. Ben
remembered Jax this morning, scrabbling
at the door, frantic to enter HQ.

Tim gave the map of Jugminster on the
wall a startled glance.

'How do we know that the rabbit
escaped?' he whispered. 'How do we know

136

that someone didn't creep out after dark and *pinch* it yesterday evening? Especially if they had a map and a *torch*!'

'Ssh!' said Ben suddenly, head cocked. 'Amy's coming!'

'Mind you, we don't *know* that's what happened!' Tim muttered hurriedly. 'I mean, we haven't got any proof! That wool could just as easily've come off Amy's jumper!'

''Course it could!' said Mini in relief. 'It's always leaving fluff around, that jumper!'

Amy's footsteps were drawing closer.

Ludo spoke with great decisiveness.

'There's no way we'll ever know, is there? So we can't put anything in the club notebook. Case unsolved, I'd say.'

They heard Amy coming up the steps.

'Quick, Lu, give me that!' said Ben, grabbing the golden fluff from him.

Ben opened the back window and let it go. He watched as a breath of wind carried it away. As he did so, Amy was just coming in through the door. She was carrying a packet of biscuits and looking very bright-eyed.

'Mum and I have been talking about what he said at lunch-time. How we won't

137

ever see his like again. And we won't, will we? Isn't it sad? About Mr Amazing. Wasn't he wonderful?'

'He was brill!' said Tim.

Ben turned round from the window, smiled and caught her eye.

'Magic, Amy,' he said.

In the same series

BOYS V. GIRLS AT JUG VALLEY JUNIORS

When Peter Pay's bike vanishes from Jug Valley Juniors, Tim Dalladay and his friends form the Handles and promise to track down the thief. 'This isn't girls' stuff,' they tell Tim's twin sister, Amy, and her best friend. 'It needs boys to handle it.'

As a joke the girls call themselves the Spouts, but the disappearance of Mrs Dalladay's bike from outside Tesco in broad daylight gives them a serious quest of their own.

And so the junior school detectives go into action – mostly against each other. Yet they should be working together if they want to avoid danger.

THE HEADMASTER'S GHOST AT JUG VALLEY JUNIORS

Tim, Amy and the rest of Handles & Spouts can't believe that Mr Morton, the headmaster of Jug Valley Juniors, would have shouted and thrown biscuits at some of the parents at the open evening. He's always been popular and respected. Now, despite his claim that he hadn't even been there, he could face the sack.

Could it have been a ghost everyone saw that evening? A poltergeist? Handles & Spouts are determined to find out in the second exciting story of this thrilling series.

HANDS UP! AT JUG VALLEY JUNIORS

Ben couldn't guess the trouble he would cause when he accidentally kicks Charlie Smith's old football into the rector's garden.

When Ben and his friends in Handles & Spouts search the garden after school, there's no sign of the ball. They get Charlie a new ball, but Charlie is desperate to find the old one.

Who can have taken the old ball, and why does Charlie want it back so badly? Handles & Spouts have some surprises in store in the third story of this fantastic series.

THE PHOTOFIT MYSTERY AT
JUG VALLEY JUNIORS

Esme asks the members of Handles & Spouts to watch the house she and her father used to live in. It's been empty since her father left for New Zealand to get a better job, and she moved in with her aunt. Missing the old times terribly, Esme has been back to the garden to stock up her bird-table. And a shadow appears at the upstairs window . . . is someone daring to make use of the house?

Handles & Spouts decide to piece together a photofit description to identify the mysterious person in the fourth brilliant adventure of this exciting series.

POISON PEN AT JUG VALLEY JUNIORS

Everybody at Jug Valley Juniors is eager to win back the Jugminster Shield from Minster Juniors, especially Tim, Amy and the others in Hands. Tim desperately wants a place in the boys' soccer team, but somebody, somewhere, is out to destroy his chances with some spiteful anonymous notes. If Handles & Spouts can't find out who it is and stop them, Tim's hopes – and the Jugminster Shield – may well be out of reach. See if you can unravel the mystery before Hands in this fifth exciting Jug Valley Juniors story.

'Far better than the run-of-the-mill adventure story'
– *The Good Book Guide to Children's Books*

ME, JILL ROBINSON AND THE TELEVISION QUIZ

Moving to Haven is full of unexpected excitements for the Robinson family. But for Jill, making friends with the high-spirited daughter of the town's mayor makes it all worth while.

However, Melinda isn't everyone's favourite person, least of all her father's. So when she gets the chance to compete in a television quiz, she really hopes that at last he will be proud of her. But it isn't that simple.

ME, JILL ROBINSON AND THE SEASIDE MYSTERY

Keeping an eye on her younger brother Tony certainly makes the Robinsons' seaside holiday an exciting one for Jill. Why does he keep disappearing on his own, and who is his new friend, Sam? Dad gets more and more angry with Tony, so Jill and her best friend Lindy try to solve the mystery, only to find themselves in real trouble!

ME, JILL ROBINSON AND THE CHRISTMAS PANTOMIME

Jill's sister, Sarah, is helping Roy Brewster produce the Youth Club's Christmas panto and Jill is dying for a leading role. It looks set to be great fun for Jill and Lindy, until the Runcorn boys get involved and spoil it for everyone. But Jill discovers that their leader, Big Harry, isn't as tough as he makes out.

ME, JILL ROBINSON AND THE
SCHOOL CAMP ADVENTURE

When Jill and Lindy start looking after a stray dog at the school camp on a remote Scottish island, the scheming Rita is determined to get them into trouble and Miss Rawlings threatens to take Cu away from them. But when Rita goes missing on the mysterious island it is only Cu who can find her.

ME, JILL ROBINSON AND THE
PERDOU PAINTING

Jill is really excited when Polly Pudham invites her home for tea because 'Pud' lives in the most expensive road in Haven. But why is Jill so interested in the painting Polly's father has just bought? And what happens when Jill's sister goes to the Pudhams' cocktail party to see the painting – what is she *supposed* to have done?

ME, JILL ROBINSON AND THE
STEPPING STONES MYSTERY

Feelings in Haven Youth Club run high when it is decided how to spend its hard-earned money. Not everyone is in favour of Roy Brewster's cracking idea to transform the river at the stepping stones bend . . . Then the bridge-building project is sabotaged! But who could have done it? Sir Harry, the local landowner, Jill's brother, Tony, or perhaps someone from the club? Jill and Lindy are determined to find out.

By Alan Davidson

The ANNABEL books

'Sparkling Annabel comedies . . . a kind of female William' – *Guardian*

'Hilarious . . . really good fun' – *BBC Radio*

'Annabel books are infectious fun' – *Birmingham Post*

A FRIEND LIKE ANNABEL

Five stories of Annabel Fidelity Bunce of the Third Year at Lord Willoughby's School, Addendon, in which, assisted by best friend, Kate, she becomes a duck's mother; by deadly detection exposes a most unexpected criminal; finds a dream partner (maybe) for the Third Year Disco; brings peace to Addendon; and trifles with her family history.

JUST LIKE ANNABEL

Annabel exposes some extraordinary goings-on at Addendon Court, home of the wealthy Franks-Walters' – and adopts a New Attitude to Life.

EVEN MORE LIKE ANNABEL

'There'll be a reign of terror,' Annabel predicts when the *repellent* Julia Channing is made a monitor.

THE NEW, THINKING ANNABEL

Three stories in which Annabel attempts to apply thought to her actions.

LITTLE YEARNINGS OF ANNABEL

What's the *real* reason, Kate wonders, for Annabel's desperate attempts to get into the Guinness Book of Records?